Exar
brok
accu
A
ques
more
same
genius
That
Reunic
now c
recall
Adle
respe
inisce
going
U
he
story
with
suffe
ness c
these
A
fror

CLASS REUNION

FRANZ WERFEL

CLASS REUNION

1929

SIMON AND SCHUSTER, INC.

NEW YORK

Translated by
WHITTAKER CHAMBERS

Against the superiority of another there
exists no weapon or remedy save love.

GOETHE, *The Elective Affinities*

CHAPTER I

THE examining magistrate, Dr. Ernst Sebastian, extinguished his half-smoked cigar. It was his custom not to smoke during office hours, and there was still one case to be heard. It was nearly six o'clock and the sun's rays struck more and more obliquely across the examination-chair, which hulked in front of his writing-table like a stricken man. Sebastian was anxious to hasten matters.

Besides, he had solemnly promised Burda, Johann Burda, the instructor at the Gymnasium, not to stay away tonight on any account. It was pathetic to see how eager Burda was about the success of that utterly unnecessary and hollow celebration. A sentimental man, who had quite imperceptibly exchanged the student's for the teacher's desk, was this mild-eyed Professor Burda. The epistolary style, in which he requested the former schoolmate "to honor the twenty-fifth jubilee of the Class of 1902 of Nikolaus Gymnasium with his presence," could hardly be called Ciceronian.

Firmly resolved not to be present on class-day, Sebastian had at first left the letter unanswered. But then Burda had appeared in person, begging his assent with naive eagerness. To refuse so pressing a request would have been discourteous. And there was a certain listless curiosity mixed in the business, though Sebastian had not at first detected it.

1

Doctor Sebastian was a man in whose mind the idea of "change" played a great part. The change from sleeping to waking, from the service back to civil life, from holiday to every-day, required much time and was bound up with many grave considerations. Even today at least two hours would be taken up by the wearisome business of changing. The first moments in any social intercourse, the entering of any drawing-room, however friendly, the salutations, the hand-kissing, the easy conversation, the assumed composure —all required the whole of a man, even in accustomed surroundings. How much more rested ought the nerves to be when one was preparing to meet again a flock of aging men who, for no good reason, would call one another by their first names.

Sebastian rang impatiently and gave orders for the accused to be brought in. Meanwhile he glanced over the statement of the case. It was headed, "Murder of Klementine Feichtinger, Prostitute." The affair was very unclear in his mind. But perhaps this lack of clarity arose from the fact that he had not prepared himself properly on this case. He was no longer certain whether it was some outer force or an inner reluctance that had prevented his studying it the day before.

Fortunately, this was the first interview he was to have with the suspected man.

Sebastian was a very modern jurist. He held that no power on earth could lift the natural state of war that exists between judge and defendant. Still, as one of the antagonists, namely the judge, possesses the more powerful weapon, it is only humane for him to allow the other a slight advantage. He went even so far as to maintain to his disapproving colleagues that the judge must permit a part of his forces to fight on the side of the enemy, that this is not only in the interest of justice, but even more necessary to the discovery of the truth. The little, approved methods of investigation—cross-examination, entangling questions, contradictions, surprise attacks—all of these he hated from the bottom of his heart. He damned them all as the *malleus maleficarum*, the reactionary witches' hammer, the rack-rule of the modern judicial system.

Ernst Sebastian cherished certain convictions which he had often propounded in technical journals on criminology.

For example, the "first hearing." In his opinion, this ought to take the form of an informal conversation. Judge and accused must learn to have confidence in each other, before any further useful progress could be thought of. But confidence could exist only when the judge sincerely acknowledged human equality. A human meeting of both parties—of both, note well—must take place, in order that the crystal of truth might evolve from the relation between the law's defender and the lawbreaker.

Although the duties of an examining magistrate were not too greatly valued, Sebastian cherished a veritable passion for his work. A hundred times he might have been promoted to higher positions. He was forty-three years old, a Landesgerichtsrat, with a higher title awaiting him, but he had managed to avoid every promotion in office. Criminal investigation was a post for younger men. In judicial circles it was commonly believed that any sharp-witted police commissioner sufficed for the job. Sebastian thought differently. A few months previously, the Minister of Justice had sent for him personally, to induce him to change his mind. In vain. People gossiped. They said Sebastian's lack of ambition was nothing but pride. During the period of the monarchy, Sebastian's father had adorned the highest judicial position in the state—that of presiding justice in the supreme court. His son was a clever man, he moved in the best society, and he was a welcome guest in many of the old Austrian palaces. With that he was content.

The judge glanced toward the door and rose from his chair. It was one of his principles to receive the prisoner as one would a guest—standing.

The prisoner was admitted. He gave the impression of being a man at least ten years older than Sebastian. He did not advance far into the room, but stood with his body sagging at the knees, and with bowed head, an attitude which the judge readily recognized as the one assumed by persons who for the first time found themselves in this situation.

Sebastian waited until the guard had left, and then, in a clear voice, the assumed metallic tone of which immediately changed to one of consideration and kindness, said:

"Good day. Are you Herr Adler?"

He extended his hand. The man with the bowed head did not notice it. Sebastian did not withdraw his hand, however, but laid it, as though his all-too-obvious gesture had had no other intention, on the outermost edge of his desk. His voice sounded casual and muted:

"Come closer, Herr Adler. My name is Doctor Sebastian."

The accused did not stir.

The judge spoke again, quickly and gently:

"We meet here today, Herr Adler, only that we may get

to know each other a little better. Have no fear. As you see, our conversation has no witnesses. My secretary is not present, and it is after office-hours. You may speak freely. Before the law you are liable only for those statements which have been duly drawn up and signed by you. I can see that you have a mistaken idea of my purpose—of the purpose of an examining magistrate. I am not your enemy. My task is not to convict, but to investigate. I can only become your enemy when I am convinced that the present grounds for suspicion are decidedly against you. But I am entirely unconvinced of that, Herr Adler. I beg you to consider carefully what I am saying. I have not the slightest interest in constructing evidence against you. Other men would probably impress upon you the benefits that a fearless confession entails. I reject any such proposals. You can rest assured that I do not see in you a guilty man, but a human being who has fallen into a difficulty of some sort. So, courage, Herr Adler! Please be seated."

Adler slunk softly to the examination-chair and sat down. The first thing about him that impressed Sebastian was his large, bald head, bumped and ridged like a worn-out pot. The crown of hair fringing the bald spot consisted of rather long, dirty-gray locks. He had a round beard, likewise gray. His forehead was so beetling that it seemed to over-arch his double-lensed glasses, behind which were lashless eyes, suffering from inflammation of the lids. The man was neither tall nor short, neither well nor poorly dressed.

Doctor Sebastian rummaged about in the collection of masks he had accumulated during his experience as a judge, endeavoring to place the man. A night-editor of some kind, he decided. Then he took up the page of the docket on which Adler's nationality was indicated. The judge's nasal twang could not quite conceal his ironical jocularity, arising from the omnipotence of his position.

"You must accept a few formalities into the bargain, Herr Adler." And he read off,

"Franz Josef Adler, born on the seventeenth day of April, one thousand eight hundred and eighty-four, at Gablonz in Bohemia. . . ."

He laid the page down slowly.

"Are you only forty-three years old? But that's just. . . ."

He swallowed the rest of the sentence in order not to hurt the accused man's feelings.

What he had meant to say was, "Just as old as I"; and he ran his hand through his thick hair and fingered his youthful cheeks. Then he pushed the docket to one side and put his questions without further preliminaries.

"Would you mind telling me about your education, Herr Adler?"

The accused had a remarkable voice. It thrust out the words and, at the same moment, swallowed them again. The sibilants dominated and gave his words a quality of odd dignity, not unlike the jerky, near-sighted bows which he occasionally appended to his sentences. His face was a picture of desperate politeness, and it reddened often and without reason. Even the skin, under his thin eyebrows, was red, and the powerful brow displayed large, sharply-outlined blotches. Sebastian observed all this, even though he did not like to peer too closely into the face of the suspected man. He perceived that, for all its desperate politeness and odd dignity, this face was grinning in a weird sort of way, as though it were seeking a companion who would find it as ridiculous as it found itself.

Adler began:

"I attended the Gymnasium. Unfortunately, I was compelled to interrupt my studies. Later I made up a good deal and took several semesters of philosophy at the University of Berlin, as well as historical subjects. I did not take a doctor's degree, however."

A jerky bow.

Sebastian evinced respect.

"Your education will be in your favor, Herr Adler. But now tell me a little, please, about your occupation. How do you live?"

Adler chewed his words meditatively.

"I live by puzzles."

Sebastian listened attentively to this paradoxical sentence before asking in bewilderment:

"By puzzles? What do you mean by that?"

Slowly Adler turned back his coat-collar and pointed to a pin. It showed a large, gold question-mark on a blue field.

"I am secretary of the Puzzle Club."

Perhaps this explanation offended the judge. Something cold and sinister crept into his voice.

"Very mysterious. But I asked you about your occupation."

"I know, Sir. I construct puzzles for the newspapers."

Doctor Sebastian took up a pencil and began to scribble and draw lines on the blotter before him.

"Very well. You construct puzzles, cross-word puzzles,

alphabet-puzzles, charades, riddles in prose and verse. I understand. But tell me, Herr Adler, is this puzzle-making a very profitable business?"

"In my circumstances," Adler said obsequiously, emphasizing his sibilants, "I require very little. Besides, I also work on chess-problems."

For a long time Sebastian considered the design he had drawn on the blotter. He began to elaborate it, to embellish it. He did not look up.

"Tell me one thing more. You resort to prostitutes quite frequently, do you not?"

Adler shrugged his shoulders and made a motion with his hands, as who should say, "Look at me, what else am I to do?"

The judge's ready smile made it clear that he understood and knew how to pardon everything.

"You need have no fear of telling me the truth about this matter, Herr Adler," he said. "We are talking as one man to another. Moreover, we are educated, modern men. I can see no cause for shame in these things. Everyone has to deal with them. One man is married, another a Don Juan; one is sensual, another lacks temperament; one is forward, another shy. I beg you to speak frankly."

The confession did not come from the accused as readily as had the request from the judge.

"Yes," he admitted after a while, "now and again I do visit prostitutes."

"Do you prefer street-women or regular houses?"

"It is quite indifferent to me, your Excellency."

Sebastian considered where he had intended the last question to lead. It had slipped his mind. He found it necessary to beg pardon again of the object of his curiosity, but of course these questions had to be.

"And how about your faithfulness, Herr Adler? Do you keep the same girl for a long time, or do you change often?"

Adler, apparently afraid that the words concealed a trap, gave an evasive answer.

Still Sebastian did not look up. Besides, it was one of his principles at these first informal hearings never to confuse his antagonist by glances, especially when the conversation touched on the heart of the case.

"But you will admit, Herr Adler, that you have been well-acquainted with the Feichtinger girl for a long time."

Adler did not hesitate a moment.

"I met her only three times. Twice in her own room—unfortunately," he added, with a pathetic gesture.

Sebastian went on scribbling.

"Pardon my asking, Herr Adler. It does not entirely pertain to this affair, and yet in a way it does, but have you never had a wife—I mean, a woman that you loved, someone really your own, someone different from these women?"

Adler kept silent.

Sebastian was about to let the question drop, when the answer came.

"No, I have never had other women than these. Why should I?"

"And when, if I may ask, did this peculiar passion of yours for prostitutes begin?"

The voice of the accused man, with its tone of odd dignity, rose somewhat.

"I do not know whether or not it is a peculiar passion. It simply happened in the course of my life, the first time while I was still a student at the Gymnasium."

Suddenly Doctor Sebastian exclaimed, "Impossible!"

He had not, however, addressed this word to the accused man, but to the blotter on his desk.

On the blotter were two words, scribbled by his straying hand. These words constituted nothing more surprising than the name of the prisoner, though in inverted order: not "Franz Adler," but "Adler, Franz."

The old Austrian schools, official and electoral lists, and registers were accustomed to give names in alphabetical order, the given name last. Perhaps this usage still obtains today. Sebastian's hand had merely obeyed the old custom when it wrote, "Adler, Franz."

The examining magistrate tore the blotter from its holder, crumpled it up, and threw it into the basket. Then, while the nervous excitement of his speech grew more and more pronounced, he said to the accused, "Tell me in detail, please, how you made the acquaintance of Klementine Feichtinger."

Cautiously Adler began to build up his story. After every sentence he made a long pause, as though he had to test the ground of his statement step by step, to see if it would hold. He tried to read the effect of his words in the features of the judge, but he saw only the signs of an unusually intense distraction.

Sebastian did not hear a word of the story.

With dramatic fitness, the rays of the gold-clouded sunset shone glaringly on the examination-chair. They laid bare the ravages in the face of this forty-three-year-old man, who seemed already aged. His forehead, his bald head, with its bumps and hollows, flamed in the flood of reddish light. Even the fringe of hair seemed afire.

Sebastian was going over and over the same thing:

"Red hair! Of course, his hair is red! The basic coloring is unmistakably a rusty red. Eyebrows lacking. Extraordinary near-sightedness. But what are even all these compared with . . ."

And he was astonished at the unexpected words that came into his mind.

"What are all these compared with that piercing flame?" . . .

He immediately interrupted the accused man's statement.

"So your name is Franz Adler?"

Adler looked at him, terrified. Caution! Was this a shot from ambush?

"Of course, your Excellency," he stammered. "Why?"

Sebastian laughed lightly. His hand moved to the bell and pressed the button.

"I am going to excuse you for the present, my dear Herr Adler. Thank you very much, but this is enough for today. Monday morning we will take up the affair with fresh energy. We have all Sunday in which to rest and think. Rest yourself and think well, Herr Adler. Thank you."

He gave him his hand, which the prisoner, with the meek irresolution of the abased, grasped limply. But he had not quite reached the door when the judge called after him again:

"Adler!"

It was the first time that Sebastian had said "Adler" and not "Herr Adler."

The accused shrank together and did not turn completely around:

"Did you want something?"

Sebastian leaned forward.

"How long have you been in the city?"

Adler reflected a long time, in his distrustful way, before he replied, "I? For about two years."

"So you came back about two years ago?"

Adler was standing facing the door. He answered indifferently, "Yes, two years ago."

But Sebastian lifted two fingers of his right hand to his nose and stared intently at the floor, as though he had just learned something of unlimited significance. Then he drew himself up and injected the official tone into his voice.

"If you have any troubles, Herr Adler, you know I am the proper person to come to."

The examining magistrate listened at the door until the footfalls of the guard and the prisoner had died away down the long corridor. Then he went to his writing-table and, following a dreamy inspiration, pulled open all the drawers. A litter was disclosed, a dusty medley of discarded official notes, of private writings and correspondence. All this paper emitted a smothering wave of nausea and hopelessness. Sebastian suffered from a painful inability to part with anything written. It was very difficult for him to tear up an old letter, a memorandum, or even a letter which he had answered. He cast a hasty glance into the gloomy hell of papers, then pushed the drawers shut. This chaos would never be sifted, ordered, or got rid of.

Sebastian's hands had become quite dirty with the accumulated dust of years. He went to the wash-basin. There he stood motionless for a long time. But instead of turning on the water, he suddenly took his hat from the rack, and, as though he could not stand it any longer, left the courthouse with unusual haste.

CHAPTER II

WHEN Sebastian entered the private dining-room of the Adria-Keller, most of the alumni had already gathered for the celebration.

A photograph, showing a group of boys posed in a sort of squat pyramid, was circulating from hand to hand. The writing under the picture stated that these three rows of crouching, sitting, and standing youths were the Graduating Class of 1902 at the Imperial Academy of St. Nikolaus.

In one way or another, time had made all the figures in this aging photograph rather ridiculous. Either they seemed to be sprouting out of their clothes or else their clothes were too big for them; and they sat there looking very much like over-frosted cakes.

A motley array of peasant hats and sailor and sport caps added to their amusing appearance. One enterprising small boy had on a kind of derby, which used to be known as a "melon"; and, for twenty-five long years, the photograph had preserved the crease with which, in that far-off hour, his boyish finger had spoiled its shape.

The picture was blotched and faded. The glossy, yellowed paper seemed to have that pallor, that suggestion of a bad complexion, which so often characterizes boyish faces.

And surely not even an expert could have attributed the right boy's face to each of the gentlemen celebrating their past youth in this room tonight.

Sebastian had to search quite a while before he found the strange youngster who had once been himself. He was standing in the third row, just behind the teacher, Professor Kio, who was seated in the middle of the group, gnawing his underlip with military fierceness.

What a thoroughly unattractive boy, thought Sebastian. The affected tilt of his head, the extreme paleness of his cheeks, his extraordinarily thin nose—all combined to make an unpleasant impression upon him. How fortunate it is that we grow old, he thought, that our features are continually being obliterated by that little hour-to-hour death! We should never let ourselves be photographed.

Sebastian was still trying to discover the face of one other boy in the photograph, when it was taken from his hand.

Professor Burda greeted him with warmth. His gentle face was beaming, as he tripped hurriedly from one group to another in the room. He seemed radiant with the sheer joy of seeing them all again. Probably he was the one man present who had no animus, no reservations to conceal. He was also the one man present who might really be said to be properly dressed for the occasion, dressed, that is, in the rather comfortable cloak of an innocent mind. The impression he made on Sebastian was that of a worried steward, who, at some sumptuous feast, is about to signal the trumpeters to announce the beginning of the revelry.

Of the twenty-seven former students of the Class of 1902, only fifteen had appeared. Three had declined the invitation; three could not be located; and six were dead. Burda lost no time in imparting these statistics to the assembled alumni.

"Still, there are more than enough here as it is," Schulhof, the actor, and director of a large German metropolitan theatre, whispered in Sebastian's ear. And, indicating Burda, with a look of amusement in his eyes, he reversed the old saw, *"Non vitae sed scholae discimus."*

Sebastian shook hands with many of his fellow guests, and more than once had to feign a gleam of friendly recognition; but the majority of them he remembered without any difficulty.

Ressl still retained his air of well-fed luxury. Faltin too was pretty much unchanged. His round, soft, black eyes roved restlessly about the room, looking for an opportunity to hear or retail some choice bit of gossip.

Then a lean figure approached Sebastian, and, looking him steadily in the eyes, extended his hand. The magistrate assumed that obliging and affable expression which he was accustomed to use in official life. At the same time he was annoyed at himself for doing so, for he knew who this man was.

"I'm Komarek, Komarek," the lean person said. "Don't you remember me?"

"Why, of course I remember you, Komarek," Sebastian replied, placing his hand reassuringly on Komarek's shoulder, like an older man or a superior. But he realized at once how false and insincere the gesture was. Komarek drew back. The evening's torture had begun.

With a suppressed uneasiness that he simply could not master, Sebastian waited to see what place Burda would assign him at table. It was a decided relief when he was asked to sit at the right of the expected guest of honor. Opposite him, as next in rank, sat Karl Schulhof—or Karl-kurt Schulhof, as he had lately taken to calling himself—

the actor and director. Sebastian felt his thoughts take a sarcastic turn as he looked at the neat part in Schulhof's glossy hair and at the actor's sharp-cut features. The Class of 1902 at St. Nikolaus had produced no really outstanding personalities.

On his own side of the table Schulhof was no doubt busy with similar thoughts.

The company fell naturally into two groups, of which the second occupied by far the larger part of the table. To this group belonged all those who had gone just so far in life and would go no further—the cannon-fodder of a barren and hopeless existence. Their faces were worn and gray, and embitterment seemed actually frozen into their features. They seemed to be neither waking nor sleeping—these life-long slaves of nothingness on this joyless evening out.

Most tragic of all was "Fischer, Robert," the once highly-gifted student, who was likewise skulking there among these shades of a drab Hades. And yet there had never been a question asked in school that "Fischer, Robert," could not answer. No aorist had ever got the best of him. Never once, even in their earliest prison-days at school, had "Fischer, Robert" been tempted to use *ut* with the indicative. Sebastian had always made merciless fun of prize students in general, and of "Fischer, Robert" in particular; but in his heart of hearts he had often felt a secret admiration for Fischer's quickness of apprehension, his mental keenness and alertness.

Now the hero who used to trudge home with a bundle of home-work every night sat ignominiously at the lower end of the table—a minor city official, discussing street-car rates and the city's building program. He was talking with

Komarek, the outcast, the worst student in the class. Had it been obtuseness on Burda's part, or a flash of irony, that had seated them together?

Not only life, but even the very order of seating seemed to bring together the two extremes in the class, the negative and the positive. Nevertheless, Komarek's old spirit had not yet quite died out: some of his biting incisiveness, some of his "Catilinian fire" still remained intact. Komarek had been dreadfully poor; and so, early in his boyhood, he had perceived that God, in His unfathomable and mysterious way, had created two kinds of people—the fortunate and the unfortunate. And it is only with the former that He has much sympathy. Among the fortunate were—especially, though not exclusively—the rich. Their wealth, thought Komarek, was not measured merely by the lavishness with which they spent money, but rather by the joyous, carefree spirit with which they could afford to spend it.

It was not merely the thickly-buttered sandwiches which the rich boys brought to school in their lunch-boxes that revealed to Komarek's eyes the mysterious differences between classes in society. The neat packages, the beautiful folds of tissue and wax paper in which those sandwiches were wrapped, seemed even more significant to him.

Besides, who could ever enumerate the thousand and one little details which reveal wealth—nicely-trimmed fingernails, for instance, or a fine, soft complexion suggestive of spacious houses, wholesome food, plentiful baths, unrestrained speech, and sleep undisturbed by worries about the future?

Then, too, the rich boys had such an inimitable way of

wearing their clothes, even while seeming careless. (When a working-man wore good clothes he was always embarrassed and afraid of being found out.)

Then there was their ability to remain perfectly at ease when a question was popped at them in school! They had a kind of haughty assurance and a way of making themselves so superior that even the teacher could not manage to keep a certain note of respect out of his voice, at the same time that he was secretly planning to take vengeance on their marks.

Komarek had also observed that among this world's blessings a title counts for almost as much as riches. For example, the teacher would call on Ernst Sebastian. Sebastian would not know a word of the answer. Then Professor Kio (though he was a righteous man among the unrighteous) would merely clasp his head in his hands and say, "What would your father, his Excellency the Chief Justice, say if he knew that his son doesn't even suspect the function of the hypothetic conditional?"

What a world of respect lay in this reproach!

There were even instances where a great name was preferable to riches. A rich good-for-nothing might be told, without more ado, "to bring his father to the office." The faculty had a veritable passion for making well-to-do parents come to Canossa. But who would have dared to summon his Excellency, Chief Justice Sebastian, Knight of Portorosso, to a conference in the school office?

Of the parents of that lower group (whom, doubtless, God had also created), of Komarek's father, for example, no mention was ever made. With a feeling of considerable embarrassment, the teachers avoided noticing that Komarek also had a family that worried over the precarious future of their son.

Once only, when he was threatened with the *consilium abeundi*, the principal had said, almost against his will, "I should like to speak to some member of your family, Komarek!"

As a result, Komarek had always felt obliged to keep the stern facts of his own existence a secret from his fellow students. When the bell rang, and the other boys opened their books with their nicely-washed fingers, Komarek would already have put long hours of work behind him. It was his duty to dress his younger brothers and sisters, to prepare breakfast for his family (his parents had to go to work), and to tidy up the house.

But the blessings of good fortune were by no means exhausted with wealth and social position. God, in His mysterious way, had arbitrarily distributed not only riches, but also intelligence. Let "Komarek, August" moil and toil and labor as much as he liked, he knew that he would never understand more than a fraction of what he was studying. "Fischer, Robert," on the other hand, who sprang from circumstances very little better than his own, understood the binomial theorem the first time it was explained to him.

To the same unequal distribution of the good things of life Komarek also attributed that phenomenon which we commonly call character, those clear, inflexible, but intangible qualities in persons, which seem to create an atmosphere of respect around them. Not only character, however, but lack of character also was among the blessings of the fortunate. One needed to stand in God's particular good graces if one was to keep smiling under Kio's barrage of humiliations every day.

By the time he was thirteen years old, Komarek possessed a remarkably thorough knowledge of these blessings, though he did not possess any of the blessings themselves. His knowledge of them made of him a kind of Lucifer at St. Nikolaus. A gloomy cloud of rebellion seemed always hovering around his head. In class he had a way of meeting all questions that he could not answer with a stolidity and a silence in which he could almost be heard to grit his teeth. He looked at such times as if he knew the answer well enough, but was refusing to give it out of spite.

Many of the teachers were secretly afraid of him and his shrewd, old eyes. Only once or twice, when his cup was filled to overflowing, did Komarek jump up and shatter the schoolroom quiet with foul and abusive words. And, on these rare occasions, everyone was more than usually zealous in pacifying him again and hushing up the painful scene. The marvel is, under the circumstances, that he ever struggled through to graduation at all.

But those alumni who had expected to find in Komarek a radical, a Bolshevik, were on the wrong track altogether. It is true that even yet the rebellious schoolboy had not made his peace with the scheme of things, but he seemed to have met it half-way at least, though he had emerged from the struggle begrimed and tired, and perhaps a little indifferent. He covered his lean body with a long overcoat and wore a black necktie, as though he were in mourning.

"He looks like a socialist shop-steward from the office of

some factory where he has worked himself up to be head bookkeeper," thought Sebastian, mentally going over his appearance.

Among these men, Komarek's bitter, proletarian expression, at once humble and defiant, seemed to reawaken. "You can beat me and humiliate me," it seemed to say to life's more fortunate souls, "but I can see right through your game, for all that."

At least that was the impression it made on Sebastian whenever his eyes happened to meet Komarek's. Those eyes repelled him, even when he defended himself against them with his most impenetrable judicial manner.

On Sebastian's left sat Ressl, the rich man, the gourmand. Even as a boy, Ressl used to boast that he could tell the vintage of the costliest wines by taste, while he used to make away with a dozen oysters at one sitting. He would never think of coming to school without his lemon-colored kid gloves, which he was in the habit of removing very slowly. It was only at Uranoff's, he said, that one could really enjoy caviar and port in the morning. It was only in the private rooms at Belcredi's that one would care to take something strong—whiskey, gin, or absinthe—toward evening. Silk underwear, ties, gloves, and the like, were worthless unless they came from Balbeck and Batka. And anyone who could think of corresponding on anything but English paper with three crowns in the water-mark simply betrayed his wretched upbringing. Let the American factories flood the market with more finished and better made shoes, a gentleman wore only made-to-order shoes, which guaranteed the personal character of his footwear against prevailing fashions. For it is the function of shoes to reveal the independent taste and sensitiveness of their owner, said Ressl. The maxims and opinions with which this boy used to terrorize his schoolmates were legion.

Although he aspired to be a leader of fashion, it had been Ressl's fate to remain epicurean rather than elegant; for corpulence always stands somewhat in the way of elegance. By command of Ressl's father, a Swedish masseur daily struggled with the *embonpoint* of the beloved son. Some audacious spirits even went so far as to assert that Ressl senior, the great textile-manufacturer, used to hire a mistress for the boy once a week, out of consideration for his health. But such stories were as malicious as they were plentiful.

Fritz Ressl, now head of his father's firm, had certainly not lost any of his corpulence, though he had lost a good deal of his soft, blond hair. At present he was amiably, though with some embarrassment, observing Burda's preparations; for it was obvious that the petit-bourgeois environment repelled him. He seemed to remove his gloves rather unwillingly, feeling perhaps a certain distaste at the idea of touching the table or the knives and forks. He kept staring at Sebastian as though in search of one sympathetic soul among the company; but he could not seem to force a conversation with the reticent judge, whose impenetrable manner became more formidable from moment to moment.

By a singular transposition, the old relations of the classmates seemed to have been resumed for the brief duration of this gathering. Ressl had always felt the most profound respect for Sebastian's name and his father's reputation.

Absurd as it might be, after twenty-five years, during which the world had witnessed change after change through war and revolution, Ressl still felt this old ridiculous respect. It was even stronger now, perhaps, than before. He, Ressl, was a captain of industry, the master of banks and corporations, and one of the wealthiest men in the country, and yet he could not help feeling uncomfortable in the presence of this underpaid civil servant.

Perhaps it was not entirely possible to annihilate the old system of values, after all. Yet what did any honorary title, minister, ambassador, or anything else mean today? Ressl used to say time and again that he, "as a big business man, dealt with life," whereas a diplomat, a civil functionary, or a judge knew nothing at all about it. And yet what comfort was there in that? The ability to deal with life did not appear to be the goal of goals after all. Although he was a business man, here was Ressl struggling to begin a conversation with Sebastian, a civil servant, presumably unable to deal with life.

Ressl knew that the Revolution had not annihilated the inner circle which we call Society: it had made Society still more aloof and inaccessible by impoverishing it. He had heard that Sebastian was a prominent figure in Society. When Ressl invited certain exalted persons to a reception in his palace, they always seemed willing enough to accept his hospitality. They drank liberally of their host's champagne and treated him with a friendly nonchalance, and yet they never showed any particular haste to entertain him in their own houses. "You've become a snob like all the rest of them," the manufacturer thought, as he smiled toward his silent neighbor, waiting eagerly for the slightest sign of recognition.

Faltin, the lawyer, who was sitting diagonally across the table from him, greeted Sebastian with a torrent of news and gossip. He did not seem to be meeting Sebastian for the first time in decades, but plunged in as if they were resuming a recently-interrupted conversation. Names of persons, dates and sums, tumbled one after another at random from his wide and formless lips. Faltin, at least— Faltin, the omniscient—had remained true to his own nature. He bubbled over with information on all branches of human activity. To be sure, his information was not always as accurate as it was vehement; but is there any real reason for accuracy when an inexorable passion is driving a man to describe the wild tumult of existence, for the edification of friends and acquaintances?

Faltin honestly strove to have an opinion about everything that happened in the world. But even the most talkative man in the world is only a man after all. So there were moments when even Faltin, in the course of his rapid reports, found himself with nothing further to tell his partner at table. At one such moment of unbearable silence, he suddenly said:

"What do you think? While I was walking through the park the other day, I met Arimondi, the opera-singer. . . ."

Sebastian objected, with some astonishment, "But that's impossible, Faltin, Arimondi's been dead for years!"

Faltin merely stared, without showing too much surprise, into his neighbor's face and nodded.

"You don't say so," he observed. "Now that you mention it, he did look rather bad."

Incidents of this nature showed plainly enough that Fal-

tin was no mere liar, but was rather consumed with an overweening desire to impart the amazing occurrences of this
world to his fellow men.

God only knows what astounding fact he was reserving
for his master-stroke, when the highly cultured voice of
Karlkurt Schulhof, the theatrical producer, took over the
conversation.

Schulhof, the artist, who knew the world and the great
men of the world, felt more than any of the others, perhaps,
how completely he had outdistanced his former comrades.
He had assumed that manner of patient superiority and
good-natured forbearance which grown-ups use with children.   He had confided to Burda that solely for the
purpose of attending this celebration he had interrupted
his trip to Italy, where he was going to make a film.   He
hinted that even here he would be compelled to spend
twenty-four hours or so in business cares and arrangements.
Never once had Schulhof confessed to himself the secret
concern that he felt for the effect which his success in the
world would have upon his former schoolfellows and on
the city in which he had grown up.   He was accustomed to
look down somewhat upon this city and these people.

But tonight he saw clearly that neither his success nor his
growing reputation had ever troubled this society of mediocre merchants, civil servants, and clerks.   His triumphs had
been achieved in a realm miles removed from the consciousness of these good citizens.   He doubted if even one out of
all those present had ever read his essay on "The Principles
of a New Dynamic" or his "The Stage as a Problem in
Space."   Probably not one of these men had ever heard a

word of his tremendous success all over Germany, or his epoch-making production, "Leonce and Lenas" at Lauchstädt. Daily these people plowed faithfully through the leading article in their favorite newspaper. With foreheads attentively wrinkled, he imagined, they scanned the financial section and the jury-lists, but glanced hurriedly over the theatrical and literary sections.

At some time or other in their youth, a few of them had written poetry and dramas, had killed whole nights with philosophic talk, and dreamed of great futures. Those were the days when he, Schulhof, had had to stand aside for a Sebastian. But what was Sebastian today, when you stopped to think of it? A conceited little judge, with puckered lips, the image of a dozen others. Time alone reveals real talent, thought Schulhof; and it was fairly safe to assume that he had been the only real genius in the class.

Indeed, he had gone so far beyond his former schoolmates that he found it impossible to discuss the fine points of his art with them. Against his own inclination, he was compelled to stoop to the more popular methods of the majority, to make himself agreeable.

He did so by relating, loud enough to be heard by the group of clerks, who were straining their ears to catch every word at the lower end of the table, what pleasant conversations he frequently had with the President of the Republic. He mentioned, too, in passing, that he stayed a number of times every year at Koburg Castle as the guest of the theatre-loving King of Bulgaria, who was one of his closest friends. In all modesty (the way in which Sebastian was listening made Schulhof somewhat uncomfortable) he felt obliged to tell them how the Ambassador at Paris insisted that no one else but himself, together with a certain international celebrity, should take charge of the good-will festivities.

But what he valued most, perhaps, were his confidential, his almost paternal relations with the great dramatic artists of the day. Let any prominent theatrical star find himself balked by some artistic problem, in the end he would come to Karlkurt Schulhof for advice: there was nothing else for it. And Schulhof was the man to give him the advice he needed. "Max," he would tell this mighty man, at whose voice even the directors trembled, "Max, you're a big man, but you can't change an author's meaning. That's vanity. Let us never forget the sacred duty that we owe to a work of art, even if it's only a pot-boiler."

By the time Schulhof had worked himself up to the point where he intended to expound his philosophy of art to these gentlemen, a little ripple passed through the gathering, and everyone rose in unison, with a rasping noise, exactly like a class in school.

The little old man who had just entered the room was bowed almost double with sickness and age. Clinging to Burda's arm, he was ushered through the door by two uniformed attendants.

Professor Voivode (geography and history) was a veteran, a survival of the faculty which had piloted the generation, now celebrating, through the regulation studies.

The old man, half-blind, smiled in bewilderment at all the strange faces, those care-worn and joyless forty-year-old faces, on which the aging organs of alimentation and circulation had already begun to plant unmistakable distress-signals. On Voivode's pale and withered face there was a different kind of indication. His resigned smile, which seemed to beg pardon of all the world for being able to say, "I'm still alive," that chin hanging down as though its owner were laboring for breath in some deep sleep—were both of them pathetic, but inexorable, Hippocratic signs. A few months, or even a few weeks, from now, and it is doubtful whether Professor Voivode, teacher of geography and history, would be able to spend the evening with his former pupils.

Now, however, when the old man entered, a remarkable change came over these pupils. They seemed to have rolled back a quarter of a century of time, and to have become students again. The change was revealed in their uneasy whispers, in a sudden embarrassment that seized them. They showed it, too, in the way each one strove to bring himself to his old teacher's attention, and in the way they addressed him only by his title.

Voivode had to shake many hands, one after the other. Awed by so many big and noisy men, he managed to stammer out a few friendly words in a squeaky voice.

Ten thousand students had passed through his class during his fifty years of service. They formed a restless, seething horde, chattering, stamping, playing pranks, and plotting mischief, in the rows of green benches under his eyes.

Eight years, and then another eight years!

For children, eight years are an eternity. But what are eight years to an old professor? Eight years, and then another eight years! André's school-atlas, the topographical maps, green and brown, the political maps, all colors! Eight years, and then another eight years! The northern calcareous Alps, the primal Alps! Granite, gneiss, and mica-slate! The Battle of Cannæ, the Peace of Westphalia, the struggle over the Investiture! The War of the Spanish Succession! Restless rows of green benches! A confusion of naughty, ink-stained, boyish hands! In the courtyard below, a hand-organ was playing the sextet from *Lucia*. . . . Eight years. . . .

Faces of children he might have recognized again. But these strange, over-exuberant, noisy men! My God, my God, if he could only manage to hold out to the end! The room began to reel. Perhaps his housekeeper had been right in not wanting him to go out that night. Voivode smiled feebly, and kept whispering, "A great pleasure, gentlemen, a great pleasure!"

Finally—and it was high time—Burda led the exhausted old man to his place of honor.

There he sat, more at ease now, although every eye in the room was fastened on him. The eyes of Fischer, the prize student, suddenly grew self-conscious and seemed to avoid his glance. Komarek's were as penetrating and quizzical as ever; Sebastian's, attentive.

Faltin started at once.

"As I was passing by your house yesterday, Professor," he said, "I noticed a lady there. I suppose it was your daughter. . . ."

It was a bad beginning. The old man puckered up his lips fiercely and prepared to defend himself.

"My daughter has been married for more than twenty years, Sir. I don't know where she's living now. No, no; thank God that I can live alone at last!"

Faltin withdrew abashed.

But Schulhof now sought to bring his personality to the rescue: "You keep amazingly young-looking, Professor, and spry into the bargain. You really haven't changed at all."

Voivode looked terrified.

"You are too kind, gentlemen. Unfortunately you are not telling the truth. It goes hard with an old man nowadays, even with us retired teachers. Just ask my colleague, Burda. He knows. He still gives a thought to us poor cast-off invalids. Yes, and he's the only one who does."

Schulhof was all indulgent eagerness:

"But I mean it, Professor, when I tell you that we'll celebrate the next anniversary together. I'd be willing to give my word on it. As I look at you I recall a hundred little details out of the past. I haven't forgotten a thing. And in my profession that means something, when you stop to think that I have to meet hundreds of men from all over Europe and America every day; and the most interesting and varied types of men too, if I may say so."

Ah, how friendly this well-dressed and sprightly gentleman was! Evidently life had called him to some higher station. The old man strove to find some clue to his identity. He would gladly have answered fair words with fair words. But he could think of nothing to say. Then Schulhof's face, with its clear-cut features, and the elegance of his speech did stir up certain ideas which the old man was now feebly struggling to put into words, to turn into a professorial homily, such as he had delivered a hundred times before.

"Yes," he began, "many are called, but few are chosen.

As I've always said, not every one is a Raphael who handles a brush. But now and then one meets with some pleasant exceptions."

"I'm on the stage," Schulhof interjected, and mentioned his name.

But by this time Burda had risen.

His speech was not witty. He dragged in all the jaded comicalities usual on such occasions. Still, the little pedagogue's eyes were grave with the fate of the generation that had groped its way out of the abyss of time with him. He felt really fraternal as he greeted his former schoolmates and heartily thanked the aged guest of honor for his presence on this occasion.

And was it so trifling a thing, after all, he asked, that bound them all together for eight long years, the longest years in their lives? Only creatures who live in the passing moment, only creatures devoid of memory or recollection, only empty heads, or empty hearts, or women, were unable to turn back to the past, or to understand that peculiarly masculine emotion, a backward glance at one's own youth. For manhood means continuity, and ethos is memory!

As Burda pronounced the word "ethos" the flame of a proud, philosophic conviction flashed from his eyes.

With a thoroughly academic gesture, he rested his hands on the table as he spoke, and swayed the upper part of his body back and forth, while he turned his attention to the departed members of the class.

Six out of the twenty-seven, or a little less than a fourth of the class, had departed this life, neither cursing it nor blessing it, said Burda. As mute and willing sacrifices in the World War they had gone to die with the silent mil-

lions. This computation deviated a trifle from strict mathematical truth, since one of the six had not been killed, but
had died of tuberculosis. However, as he had perished
during the War, Burda, out of pity and class-pride, did not
hesitate to ascribe to him a hero's death.

Then the speaker explained that some of the other six
absent comrades had not replied to his invitation, while
some could not be reached simply because they had never
been heard from after graduation. It was all the more
gratifying to have been able to find fifteen alumni, several
of whom were no longer living at their former addresses.

"There is our Schulhof, for instance," Burda continued,
"who used to delight our reading-circle with his talent for
imitating teachers and famous actors. Now he has made
a splendid reputation of his own in the world. I must confess that in the café I've sometimes read through a big pile
of papers simply to see his name in print and bask in a little
of his glory."

Then he mentioned each of those present, in turn, and
picked upon some eccentricity; for Burda, the ethicist, had
turned, with a sort of threadbare irony, to the humorous
part of his address. Their faces grew embarrassed and
flattered.

Sebastian heard him saying something about Ressl's
palace and the class-nabob's American automobile, the dust
of which poor Burda pretended to take pleasure in swallow-
ing. Then Sebastian could not bear it any longer, and he
struggled convulsively to benumb all his senses, so that he
need not hear anything more—so that he need not be terrified by the mention of his own name.

It was a singular condition to which Sebastian was now

a prey. If there were such a thing as mental suffocation, that designation would describe his present state of mind. A horrible, abysmal questioning of the value of life itself (though these are merely facile and senseless words) surged in a tremor over his body. But might not this stifling, this metaphysical need for air, have some physical cause? Might this not be a prelude to that heart-attack which he lay in fear of every night of his life, but which he saw inexorably coming on? Yes, something was slowly creeping up on him. Sebastian had thoughts of getting up quickly and excusing himself on the grounds of a sudden indisposition. But he could not muster the courage to do so.

So he remained sitting in that void of resounding aridities, that waste of words. Here and there on the faces of these men he detected little traces of childishness, some of the blood and milk of babyhood that had not been washed away. These vestiges increased his horror. Sebastian thought of all the millions of breaths, all the thousands of nights and days that had gone to make up one of these mediocre careers, the capstone of which was a respectable seat at a banquet such as this one.

Was there no possibility of leaping beyond it all, of crashing through the maze? Is a man too old at forty to escape the choking fogs of this broken generation, with its eternal yesterdays and its eternal tomorrows, its never-to-days, its falsities, its senselessness, its half-men? Oh, those horrible faces around him! Schulhof's subaltern conceit, Faltin's garrulity, Ressl's vast apathy, Burda's pompous gesture of simplicity, his own sly nature, and, along with them, the dull horde of the nameless. None of it had changed at all!

Was there not one single man among them?

Sebastian kept his seat and did not say a word.

They began a meal which was not particularly dainty. Two surly waiters brought in plates of bouillon in which thick rings of fat and chives were swimming. A combination salad followed, a favorite custom at the marriages of petty officials. The roast, carved into barbarous chunks, was drowned in cold gravy. A crumbling fruit-cake completed the meal. The beverages were beer and a sour, native wine.

This menu, which Burda had worked out with considerable care, was well-fitted to the economic average of the company. Everyone present had paid a small sum. But, to Burda's credit, let us reveal the fact that he had taken three of these payments on himself, so that two classmates, to whom even this small expenditure was a burden, enjoyed "exemption from the school-tax."

They did not know this, however, and thought that Ressl had paid for the whole meal. He, the gourmand, prodded his food politely but reluctantly, and whispered to the waiter to bring him something "a little less heavy." But as they had nothing that he liked, he sat in front of his plate of apple-sauce and meat, and excused himself on the score of his poor stomach.

Sebastian ate slowly and conscientiously. Burda, in the rôle of genial host, supervised everything.

Old Professor Voivode made an unforgettable picture during the meal. Death seemed hovering almost visibly above him, yet he showed an appetite rare at his age, like a greedy man who wants to eat everything up before surrendering his place to his successor. His trembling but unerring hand kept carrying larger and larger forkfuls of food to his mouth.

Perhaps it was more than appetite that he was betraying. Perhaps it was hunger. At last he deliberately selected two oranges from the fruit-dish, and, without the slightest sign of embarrassment, slipped them into the pocket of his old coat.

After the roast, an agreeable sense of unconcern set in. They began to experience that comfortable feeling which, even in mixed company and after the most dubious of meals, comes on, once the stomach-nerves and the wounded personal feelings have been lulled to rest by the process of digestion.

Even the pressure on Sebastian's temples began to relax a little. By the time the liqueur was reached, things had already progressed so far that Schulhof sprang up and, martially gnawing his underlip, shouted to Fischer, the prize pupil and minor city official:

"Fischer, Robert, translate as literally as possible, but as freely as necessary, the following sentence from our daily experience: 'The commander-in-chief captures the city.'"

Fischer rose obediently to turn the sentence into Latin. It was hard to tell whether he did so in order to carry out the actor's joke, or whether he was behaving like the old circus-horse when it hears music.

All these sedate gentlemen were overtaken by a kind of transport, as, with one voice, they shouted the portentous name, "Kio!" For he, their former teacher, whose virtue,

strength, and gentle whimsicality only the initiated knew—
he, the dæmon, to whose mystic cult only the students of
St. Nikolaus belonged—he, the good and evil spirit who had
grown out of their childhood with them—now seemed to be
hovering over their gathering. No, his spirit had entered
Schulhof; he had entered the actor's body.

Schulhof's glossy hair no longer appeared to be black.
Some mysterious current of air fanned a few wispy
gray locks on his forehead. Instead of his pearly teeth,
worn and prominent gums appeared in his upper jaw. His
cheeks, chapped from shaving, were framed on either side
by reddish and silvery sideburns. It did not matter that
Schulhof was wearing a dinner-jacket, for his hips seemed
compressed in a tight-fitting coat, and his hand toyed with
an invisible watch-chain, from which—never to be forgotten
—hung an amethyst charm.

And it was Kio, passing gloomily from one to another
of them. He strode about the room, a shrouded presence,
moving through invisible rows of benches in their old
classroom, which had somehow been transferred to the
Adria-Keller. His body, which had survived the rigorous
campaign in Bosnia and had been decorated for it, stood
erect and tall, and his voice was the one they knew of old:

"Vocables are the masonry of a language. The student
who fails to learn his vocables is a poor mason. But grammar is the mortar of language, and grammar begins with
the conjugation of the verb."

With a stamp of his foot he stopped pacing.

"Faltin!" he cried. "Stop that nonsense! You know
better than that."

Then round the class again:

"Now take the verb 'mori' and conjugate it quickly and correctly. Faltin, take 'I might have died.' Fischer, Robert, 'Let us both die.' Ressl, 'O, would that I had died!' Of course, his Excellency, Herr Ressl, as usual, hasn't the slightest suspicion of how to construe 'utinam' with the conjunctive pluperfect. His Highness, the Duke, was compelled to spend yesterday in more attractive and convivial pursuits than studying his lessons. Don't say anything, Ressl! I'm on to your sly excuses, with which you think you can make a fool out of me. As an old soldier, I'm ashamed of you. . . ."

Suddenly his eye fell on another victim:

"Komarek!"

A pause.

"Komarek, stand up when I call on you. And now, Komarek, conjugate, tense by tense, 'Hail, Caesar, those who are ready to die salute you!' "

Silence.

"I'm waiting, Komarek. I'm still waiting for your answer, but I'm tired of waiting now. . . . Do you mean to tell me that you can't do that sentence, which is one of the commonest in the schoolbooks? Why, every letter-carrier knows it, not to mention still more ordinary persons. But the *dies ater* is gathering over your head, Komarek, the cataclysm is drawing nearer. Two celestial bodies are rushing together in space. I'm warning you, Komarek, the end of the world will be more unpleasant for you than for me."

Another feverish volley of questions around the class.

"Yesterday you failed in mathematics and could not distinguish between the haruspices and the augurs. . . . You are pale, Komarek. . . . I don't know what vices you're up to now, whether you're playing billiards instead of studying, or are visiting the 'nymphs' at the theatre. But whatever the trouble is, Komarek, I'll apply the inverted subordinate clause to your case, and say that Komarek, if he continues this sort of thing, like Jugurtha, will have to shake the dust of Rome from his feet!"

Undistracted by the applause of the company, Kio-Schulhof strode to and fro, gnawing at his underlip. The actor had achieved a weird identity with his old teacher. The dead man was conjured up before his former pupils and the living were miraculously transported into the presence of the old disciplinarian.

Kio was the first and only personality they had encountered at school, and they cherished a devoted and loving memory of him. The choleric old man had filled them with terror; and yet, while the thunder of his words was still crashing around their heads, they had always been conscious of something else that soothed their fears. This something, of which they felt so sure, was love.

Terror and love: these two divine paternal characteristics in him made them deify Kio. He was a god not devoid, too, of a ridiculous quality; but this in no way detracted from him—on the contrary, it merely added a golden halo to his vigorous figure.

They fondly imagined that their Kio was a real original, forgetting that ever since the first classical academy there have always been professors who, possessed by the *furor grammaticalis,* speak with a pedantry so marked that their sentences seem translated (as literally as possible, but hardly as freely as necessary) from the classic tongues.

To be sure, this wrathful figure which had taken up its abode in the body of the actor was not to be defined solely on the basis of his grammatical peculiarities. For on countless occasions he had revealed his heart and a unique quality of fiery righteousness. Kio was the epitome of that race of officials of imperial Austria which appeared to have perished with him. At this moment they were sadly aware of all that in their school-days they had but vaguely apprehended.

Although he himself neither served nor belonged to any particular class, this Austrian of the old Empire was filled with the high dignity of a super-personal hierarchy that would tolerate no plebian arrogance. He was forever drawing "useful lessons for every-day life" from their prescribed reading in the classics. But Kio's idea of every-day life was made up of certain mysteriously stratified classes, of grades of service, of titular ranks and unalterable limits of authority.

The state played a mystical, an almost godlike rôle in his mind. In reading Livy, he always said the same thing whenever the word *sopor* appeared in the text. Explaining this word, Kio used to tell how, in the mountain-village which had been his home, the peasant women would soothe their babies with sleeping-potions, with "soporific decoctions of poppy," so that they would not be disturbed at their work in the fields.

"Who stands with a sword in one hand and scales in the other to nip such crimes in the bud?" he would ask. "It is his Excellency, the imperial district judge."

The state was sacred in his eyes: it constituted a higher order, like heaven, which might occasionally visit earth unrecognized, in order to save the sinful.

And the highest official was God. But God was an invisible presence, who could be approached only indirectly with the assistance of the higher and lower clergy.

God wore neither a civil nor a military uniform. His Royal Highness and Imperial Apostolic Majesty, the Emperor in Vienna, the next in rank to God, wore a general's uniform, with an oak-leaf on the collar, to distinguish him from the other generals.

From the Emperor, the gradations descended in uninterrupted succession down to the lowest order, which included students in their first year at an Imperial Academy.

The thousand-year-old empire would be really perfect, thought Kio in his inmost heart, only when every man in it had become a part of the state, an official, a definite point on the eternally ascending and descending scale of rank, a cog in the mystical machine.

But, of course, it would be some time before this came to pass. For within the body of the state itself, the "subversive elements" flourished ineradicably, while on the periphery of the state lurked crime, anarchy, treason, cigarette-smoking high-school freshmen, and unchaste "nymphs."

In spite of the thick fog that seemed to be stifling him, Sebastian could not help smiling at the sin-laden word "nymphs." The delicate aroma of a remote culture seemed wafted into our clamorous age with that word.

Kio was still pacing to and fro. Only Professor Voivode and Komarek did not seem impressed by this resurrection of the dead. The old man's head was growing heavier and heavier. He was struggling with drowsiness. He did not understand what it was all about. At last, with his eyes still half-open, he surrendered to sleep.

As for Komarek, he was not the man to forget an old

injury; so, though he laughed, he laughed resentfully, and looked as if he were ready to settle accounts even with the ghost of his former tormentor.

But Schulhof-Kio bent forward. He motioned the class to keep absolutely silent, as he crept up on tiptoe to catch an imaginary student napping. When he was right behind the invisible boy, he stood still and commanded:

"Continue reading Tacitus where we have just left off."

Schulhof suddenly wheeled about and transformed his body into the imaginary student. He started up out of a deep sleep and began to stammer unintelligible words. He forced his words out quickly and swallowed them again. The loud sibilants gave them an odd sort of dignity. Then he made a hesitating and near-sighted bow . . .

Suddenly Sebastian interrupted the performance by remarking slowly, "I spoke to Franz Adler today."

His voice must have sounded strange; for with one movement they all turned toward him.

Schulhof silently went back to his place.

It seemed to Sebastian as if he were sitting beside his voice; it came from his lips with an unfamiliar sound.

"Yes," he continued, "Adler was brought before me a few days ago for examination. It was Franz Adler all right. But at first I did not recognize him."

Faltin was growing excited.

"Why, it's impossible!" he exclaimed. "Adler is living in America. I know positively that Adler is living in New York. I heard it from a mutual acquaintance."

"You are mistaken, Faltin," Sebastian said quietly. "Franz Adler is living in this city. He constructs cross-word puzzles for a living. He came back two years ago. But at present he is in the custody of the investigating division of the Department of Justice."

Komarek raised his two big clenched hands.

Sebastian concluded, "He is suspected of the murder of a prostitute."

"For God's sake!" cried Burda in amazement.

An expression of terror passed over the faces of the others also.

Schulhof alone did not seem surprised. He even put on a knowing look.

"A murder!" he said. "We always said he would do something quite remarkable."

Sebastian's lips became a thin line at this remark:

"I did not state that he was a murderer. I say that he is suspected in connection with a murder."

Faltin lifted his hand to his forehead meditatively.

"Why, of course. Murder of a prostitute. The papers were full of it two weeks ago. A murder because of jealousy, at the Korea dance-hall——"

Sebastian stared at him passively.

"You are mistaken again, my dear Faltin. Klementine Feichtinger was found dead in her own room. And, until we know something more to the contrary, we are forced to assume that her last visitor was our fellow student, Franz Adler."

An uproarious discussion followed. Most of the gentlemen had jumped to their feet and were trying to outshout one another. Burda, with wide-open eyes, seemed to be gazing into the misty memories of the past.

"How is it possible for anyone to vanish so completely?" he asked. "I'm afraid that we are all guilty of a terrible neglect in this case."

But Ressl, the captain of industry, had suddenly become talkative:

"We all stuck our heads in the sand in order not to see the truth, my friend."

Schulhof was musing slowly, and making an obvious effort of it.

"For the life of me," he said, "I can't imagine how we came to lose track of him. Weren't you sick for several weeks at that time, Sebastian?"

But Burda was stubborn.

"At least we could have made some effort to find out what had become of him."

Faltin was more doubtful. "His mother died just after school closed. Where could we have found out anything?"

"In any case, it was mean and thoughtless," said Burda.

Schulhof's beautiful voice interrupted his reproach. "You know, I seem to remember Adler dimly," he said, "like an explosion of wet powder. . . . Wasn't there something like that about him?"

Ressl declared that he had always noticed traces of secret insanity in Adler. In fact, he still felt that way about him. "Wasn't he a kind of spiritualistic medium?" he asked.

Some of the others raised objections. Fischer recalled that up to a certain time Adler had always been one of the best students, and that it was not until quite late in his career at school that, for some unknown reason, he had fallen behind so surprisingly. Faltin mentioned the title of a poetic drama that Adler had written when he was only sixteen. It was strange, but no one who had once heard this drama could ever quite forget it. Some of them recalled details from his life.

"Adler was certainly a genius," Burda declared, passionately.

Sebastian contradicted him. "No sixteen-year-old boy is a genius, Burda."

Schulhof suddenly had an idea.

"It may sound foolish, I can't help it, but it suddenly occurs to me that I saw Adler a few years ago in a little village in Germany. It was half-past ten in the evening. We were playing a guest-performance. The play was over, and as I went out through the stage-door, I saw a man standing before me. He was of medium height, with thick glasses and a peculiarly shaped head, and he kept staring in my face as if he wanted to speak to me. 'Who can it be?' thought I. 'It seems to me I know that face.' I've even dreamed about that man's face since then. . . . As I said, it may sound foolish, but I'm sure now that it was Adler."

Then Faltin, who had so emphatically insisted that Adler was in America, could not refrain from following suit and announcing that he had caught a glimpse of Adler a few days before, in a crowd in the city.

All these reminiscences were like a fine dust obscuring Sebastian's recollection of the true appearance of the man in the prison-cell.

None of them believed for a minute, they said, that the dreadful accusation could be true. For, in their heart of hearts, many of them felt a troublesome sense of guilt and shame, and even of sorrow. Komarek, in his long, ill-fitting coat, stood to one side, but the others crowded around the judge.

Sebastian wanted to escape them. He said he could not tell them anything before the investigation had been completed. He would be glad to arrange a meeting with all his old classmates, and some time next week would answer all their questions. The affair had begun to make a deep impression on him also, and he hoped with all his heart that the charge against Adler would prove unfounded—in its present brutal form, at least.

He had known Adler more intimately than had any of the others, perhaps, and he knew that he could never murder anyone. Come what might, Adler's innocence was established, so far as Sebastian was concerned!

Sebastian had uttered these glib sentences in the hasty, nasal voice with which successive generations of civil servants had been in the habit of putting off petitioners. The others recognized the tone, and stopped questioning him. They turned away from him at once. But Sebastian, who all evening long had preserved his formal manner, now suddenly and involuntarily began to talk.

"You can imagine how I dread this coming Monday," he confessed.

All this time, old Voivode had been smiling with half-opened eyes at the tumult of excited voices. Suddenly he awoke. "Adler?" he said. "Did somebody mention Adler?"

Cautiously he lifted his trembling index-finger; and it seemed as if, among all these strange faces, he had at last remembered the face of one student who was not strange to

him. "Adler? Why, of course. The red-headed boy with
freckles. First row to the left."

.   .   .   .   .

Half an hour later, a little party of alumni were walking
on the far side of the river, through the streets of the
imperial old city. They were wondering why Sebastian
had fastened himself upon them. He was wondering a
little himself. Why had he not, as he had originally intended, slipped away and returned home at the first good
opportunity? He had already allowed several good chances
to slip by. But he was driven on mechanically. Any society, in any street, was better than the lonely road home.
He felt it necessary, however, to apologize for his sociability.
"We broke up our evening altogether too quickly," he said.

Schulhof, who had lived so many years away from home,
was planning to take a night-walk through the more beautiful sections of the old city. That would be the best way to
celebrate alumni-night, he thought.

They had formed a group by themselves in the old days
—Ressl, Schulhof, Faltin and Sebastian.

As if by a tacit understanding, Adler's name was not
mentioned again. It was a very clear night. The bright
moonlight exaggerated all the angles of the buildings and
transformed palaces and houses into mere empty façades,
surfaces, and planes. It seemed to lie like a thick white
powder on the ridges and in the hollows of the buildings.
The shadows were velvety. The baroque, that truly lunar
style, shone lustrous in the moonlit night.

They did not say much to one another, though Faltin
naturally uttered the names of all the former noble houses

they passed. They had long been transformed by the new republic into ministries and official buildings. In the daytime a bustling, active life went on here. But by night this quarter of the city regained some of the deathly quietude that it had guarded for so many centuries.

"It really hasn't changed at all," said Schulhof, the stranger.

The former students of St. Nikolaus Academy passed through the hushed streets as through a dream that would not return.

Before one palace-gate a long line of official cars was waiting. After all, the enchantment of these streets and buildings could last only for a few brief night-hours. They themselves belonged to a newer and stronger time.

Later, in the narrow alleys near the barracks, they saw a crouching shadow. It circled around their little group. It was an old man, in old-fashioned clothes, wearing an impossible top-hat. Even at a distance they recognized an old officer in civilian clothing. He made a few zigzag detours as though terrified, and then disappeared.

Faltin stopped short. "Do you know who that is?" he asked. "That's the notorious General Treisbacher, one of the biggest bloodhounds developed in the whole war. A member of the recruiting staff. Why, he declared the dead were fit for military service. And me, too."

The lawyer bared his pitiably thin arm in evidence of the unrighteousness of such a decision.

"Why did he run off like that?" someone asked.

"Because he's afraid. He leaves his house only at night. He has delusions of persecution and believes that the people will kill him if they find out who he is. . . ."

Schulhof made a grandiose gesture, with his hand, toward the vanishing figure. "There you are," he said. "A symbol."

Later, as they were standing in front of the barracks, peering into the court, Schulhof resumed:

"I know a story about another symbol, too, a symbol no less mad, but far more moving than the one we have just seen. At least it moved me profoundly at the time. It was some time in September, 1914. I was one of the rank and file in an infantry battalion. We were standing in this very courtyard. Later, thank God, I succeeded in deserting it for an entertainer's job behind the lines. But, at the time I'm speaking of, we were drawn up here in four companies. 'Parade rest!' commanded an officer. 'Silence!' Everyone was shouldering his own small load of woe—a knapsack, with a trench-spade and tent. There was a sudden movement in the ranks. 'Attention!' The bandmaster's baton gave the signal for the national anthem. On the other side of the wall the women began sobbing and crying. And at that moment, the other symbol passed in front of our lines, with a slow, martial stride. It was Kio! Kio in an ancient lieutenant's uniform. He had on a dark-blue military coat, slate-gray breeches, red linings, and a low peaked cap. The uniform of 1868, with a sword-knot as big as a horse's tail! The old man was marching along, 'eyes right,' and looked tremendously dignified. Everyone was a little overwrought at that time; and I know I let out a howl like a mad dog. They told me later that our symbol presented himself every day at the regimental recruiting-station and requested to be sent into the field with the next consignment of troops. Finally they forbade him to wear his uniform, and the guard at the gate would not let him in. . . ."

"So he died," Faltin finished.

"When did that happen?"

"November third, 1914," the omniscient Faltin answered.

Sebastian gazed intently at the barracks. There was no Kio to be seen. But Sebastian's ear still heard the echo of that martial step, "One two, one two." For the second time that night he felt a heart-attack coming on. Something was approaching with each of Kio's steps.

As they crossed the suspension-bridge, Sebastian thought, "It still smells of tar." He was conscious that the thing drawing nearer was the end, the end of the heart's beating, a heart-attack. His hand clutched the parapet. He did not believe he could walk another hundred steps.

Presently, however, they were all sauntering across a wide square. They had left the martial tread behind them. It echoed now very faintly, as though from a great distance.

Ressl pointed to a large building, in front of which hung a red, green, and blue electric sign, like some grotesque Christmas-tree.

"Trocadero," he said. "It used to be the Gran Canon. Do you remember?"

"It passed into the hands of the Vita Corporation some time ago," Faltin observed, and mentioned the price it had brought.

Sebastian was struggling wearily with his own thoughts. How could they say that the Trocadero used to be the Gran Canon, when one can't even be sure that Adler is the same as Adler?

Through the revolving-door, men and women poured out of the resort. The women, with their gay clothes and lovely legs, glowed like beautifully-shaded lights. The night-air was alive with their laughter, their movements, their fragrance.

Ressl's chubby, boyish face became alert. He snuffed the air. "What do you say, let's go in," he said. They saw that he did not wish to let this furlough from married life pass without making use of it.

Sebastian was picturing to himself the fruit-and-vegetable market which would be set up in the square, once the pleasure-seekers had gone home.

He was silent.

He stood stock-still, musing.

Ressl touched his arm. "You, too, used to be one of the regular habitués of the Gran Canon," he said.

It is possible that Sebastian might have chosen that moment to slip away, had he not chanced to look across the square. Komarek was passing on the other side, a gaunt, dark shadow. He bowed low to them, excessively polite, making a sweeping gesture with his hat.

The others crowded through the revolving-doors, thinking that Sebastian was following them.

But he was hastening with long strides across the square. Class Reunion was over for him.

CHAPTER III

IT was long past midnight when Sebastian seated himself once more before the writing-table in his own room. The feeling of exhaustion, the suspense which twice that evening had come over him like a mounting fever, had quite disappeared. A state of extreme wakefulness, of mental excitement, had set in, together with an unusual impulse to write, something hitherto wholly unknown to him. . . . Of course, even after he had reached his twentieth year he had written now and again, poetry and short stories. He had even thrown together a one-act play. But all his literary pretensions amounted to, as he now knew, was a certain preciosity of style and the desire to impress people.

He had always been clever enough to feel the same sense of disappointment every time his words had in some impish way changed in flowing from his pen on to the paper, and in the way they had become utterly different from what he had intended. A word, he thought, was like a badly-ridden horse in a cavalcade. It tugs at the reins, and fights, and uses every trick to take the bit in its teeth and go its own way, just as the horse, in such a case, will prance a little, and then press on after the rest of the troop without worrying much about the art of riding. Sebastian had the same luck in his poetic endeavors. His words kept straggling back to the verbal herd, to pretty phrases, and to what had already been repeated a thousand times before. And Sebastian knew it.

But what he felt tonight was something entirely new to him. It was no longer a mere question of words at all, of how to write. It was not even a question of confession or self-justification. It was an overpowering, irresistible passion that compelled Sebastian to sit down at his desk, to stir up the memory of his past life and set it down in black and white for ever. This past was striving to project itself into the present, to assume definite form, not for Sebastian's sake, nor for Adler's, but for its own.

He must obey its dictates.

Sebastian was hardly aware that he was writing. He did not stop to write longhand, but used shorthand in his breathless haste. It was full of arbitrary symbols and abbreviations that his speeding fingers invented.

He wrote, for at last he believed in his power to write.

．　　　．　　　．　　　．　　　．

It ALL began when my father exiled me from Vienna. He was not what we would call a dyed-in-the-wool official jurist, no strict letter-of-the-law man, without any broader point of view. In society, he was esteemed as a pianist. As a young man, he had worked hard to found the Richard Wagner Society. It will always seem an inexplicable contradiction to me that a man of his type, whose finest characteristic was a crystal-clear feeling for form, should be so passionately fond of sensuous music.

There was one point in his nature, however, on which he would stand for no trifling. And it was exactly here that I had offended him.

My father hated any kind of defeat. The vanquished never got any pity from him, only a cold contempt. It was simply inconceivable to him that any human being should sink under his load, should fall short of the goal that is attained by the vast majority of ordinary mortals. This clever man, so amiable about most things, suffered—or at least so it seemed to me then—from the fact that I had got through the fifth form at school only by the skin of my teeth, that I had received a zero in deportment and no more than a barely passing grade in anything else. He seemed sincerely ashamed to be the father of a son who was so unstudious, dull, and inattentive, that even with the "slight requirements of the modern schools" he could do no better than the lazy majority. It never occurred to him that I was only a boy, an immature child, who, in spite of an academic *débâcle*, might still go far in life. The difference between man and boy simply did not exist for him. He never treated me with the grown-up's ironic superiority. He did not reproach me; he made no scenes; he simply let me feel the annoyance it cost him to have to sit at table with an inferior being who certainly was no credit to the name of Sebastian von Portorosso.

But at heart he was annoyed by something quite different. He was by nature a bachelor and had no right ever to have had a son. I, too, am a bachelor by nature and would care just as little about a son as my father cared about me. (In my case, the trait is so far developed that I do not even know whether my wife, who ran away to Argentina to escape my indifference, has a child by me or not!) My father had been separated from my mother as far back as I can remember. She died when I was six years old.

My existence troubled my father. No doubt this was bound up with that almost pathologic pride with which he was afflicted, a pride that at times amounted to a complete loathing of his kind. For example, pride made him avoid as much as possible having human bodies come anywhere near him. When subordinates called at his office, he never gave them his hand. Even his sensitiveness to smells—in conversations he almost always kept his face half-averted—was nothing more than this same consuming pride. A half-grown son is always a caricature of his father. It wounded my father's pride to see himself reflected in me. At least, so it seems to me now.

After the long summer vacation, which I spent in hard study, I was sent to this city in order to take the deficiency-tests before entering a new school. And here, twenty-seven years after, I am still living. Here I lived through the downfall of the old and the birth of the new state. I have become a native here, a public official, though all this is absolutely indifferent to me.

I spent the years of my early youth in the house of two women, my father's sisters, Aurelia, a widow, and Elizabeth, who never married. They remain the tenderest memory of my life. I was the man in their house. They demanded nothing of me. They did not attempt to bring me up. They simply loved me. They were jealous of each other where I was concerned, and their rivalry flattered my vanity.

I still pass by their house every day, by that aging structure, by that gate from which the dark, ambiguous memories of my youth still seem to pour out to me. But I no longer notice the house; it has ceased to exist for me, like the city in which I have my office—like my whole life, perhaps, through which I saunter day after day as I do past that gate, in no particular haste, with a cigarette in my mouth.

But it was a great mistake to have allowed myself to be seduced by Burda into attending that gathering of gibbering monkeys, though I can't deny that I was any different from the rest of them. (I was one of the drabbest of drab ghosts.) But why go through such an evening at all? Why carry away a ruined digestion and a ruined peace of mind from an evening like that? What is the good of all that painful pretending that one is at the take-off again, when life's race was actually forfeited long ago?

I am forty-three years old. If I don't keep to my diet, I lie awake the whole night, tossing. My heart isn't worth much now either. I haven't been to a doctor about it yet, but I know. A stiff climb or any sudden exertion makes me lose my breath. The slow pain in my left arm makes me suppose that I'm a candidate for hardening of the arteries. My father died of the same disease when he was fifty-three; and I have not only inherited all his tendencies, but am an incurable smoker besides. That smothering sensation this evening, that chronic palpitation of the heart, is nothing but a premonition of my early and sudden demise. Why don't I go to a doctor? Need I then embitter the little that is left of my life by knowing the truth?

I am passable-looking, not yet old, better-looking, on the whole, than in my youth, since I now expend much more thought and money on my clothes. As I have no ties or entanglements of any kind, and have inherited my aunts' fortune, it is easy for me to look well-dressed and to keep up a rather tasteful apartment. When I was twenty years old, women seldom ogled me on the streets. Today it is quite a different story. My eyes meet many ardent, questioning, and lingering glances. When I desire, I can have women, and not by any means unattractive women; rather, women of position, women whom one would ordinarily never even suspect. But I am not given to falling in love. I do not let myself be caught that way. Caution advises me to watch my heart, whose quickened beating unnerves me at every moment.

If I suddenly feel my pulse in court, my colleagues call me a hypochondriac; but how does that help me, when I have to lie awake long nights imagining the details of death and dying?

Of course, I am fully aware that it is a matter of supreme indifference to the world and me whether I walk from my house to the court five thousand seven hundred times more —or only thirty-eight. It is a matter of complete indifference to the world and to me, and yet what a wonderful feeling of security there would be in the knowledge that I shall travel this route, say, five thousand times more.

It is a rather tiresome route, through five small and two larger streets. It takes a half-hour, and I do it on foot. I don't deny that this is one of the most important concerns of my day, although, while I am walking, I am very little interested in the life around me, and saunter along in a kind of semi-conscious doze.

I ask nothing more of life than this. I am altogether a creature of fixed habits; I don't like innovations. The thought of any change in my position—for example, the promotion which I myself have more than once prevented

—makes me shudder. Particularly when I think of the
new office that I should have to take over.

All the more reason why it was an unpardonable impru-
dence to spend the evening with men whom I had long ago
thought forgotten. But when I stop to consider it, how
could I have avoided this mistake? Eventually I should
have had to write down these recollections. However exaggerated and ridiculous it may seem, the fact is that my
encounter with Adler has confronted me in life with something to which I feel unequal. Furthermore, I don't know
exactly in what this something consists, or how I am to
prepare to meet it.

Here are two of the most superficial of the questions that
trouble me: Ought I to make myself known to Adler?
And, how can I reconcile my duty as a judge with my duty
as a human being, especially the peculiarly complex duty
involved in this case?

I marvel at the speed with which my shorthand covers the
paper. I myself do not seem to be thinking at all, I am not
writing at all. The impact of some force is driving the
words out of me. When I think of Monday, I have to grit
my teeth together in painful bewilderment. My forehead
is wet and my body burns feverishly, as though I had a chill.

I was sixteen years old when Professor Kio first ushered
me into the sixth form at St. Nikolaus Academy and presented me to my new schoolmates. I still remember the
words he said to me in his odd way before we entered the
room: "You are an immigrant. Do your best to make
yourself at home. It won't be easy."

It wasn't easy.

Everyone who has ever been through a similar experience knows how unpleasant such moments are. You sit down under a barrage of curious, appraising glances, confronted by a hostile, superior power that immediately envelops and closes over the unfortunate intruder. I stared straight at the blackboard and pretended to be unconcerned. By doing so I emphasized the bad impression that I had already made. For even then there was a black mark against me. A pupil with the taint of a deficiency-test, who changes both his school and his city, stands pretty much convicted in advance. I comforted myself with the thought that, coming from the capital, I stood higher, socially and in my experience of life, than did the students of this provincial city. In this I was mistaken. For I was soon compelled to recognize that the students at St. Nikolaus were far better read and better informed than my former schoolmates at the Schotten Academy in Vienna. In consequence I ran up against an unexpected consciousness of superiority for which I was not at all prepared.

The teacher showed me a seat in the third row on the right. My neighbor was Burda. Behind me sat Faltin, in front of me Bland, who was killed in the war.

In the first row to the left, next the middle aisle, where the instructors were in the habit of pacing back and forth while they were teaching, sat Franz Adler. He was the first pupil to attract my attention. At first I did not like him. His appearance repelled me. I suffer a great deal from the fact that the features and the physical appearance of many men turn me against them before I really get to know them. Later on I may find the same men very congenial.

For the first few days Fritz Ressl pleased me best. He was a little slow, of course, but a very attractive, fair-haired fellow, always laughing over something. Besides, he wore silk shirts and brought something new with him to school every day—gold penholders, cigarette-cases, watches—which impressed me. Then, too, he did not carry his books in a strap, but in an important-looking brief-case, which elicited my further admiration. Besides, Ressl was the first to speak to me. He was the person least strange to me in my strange surroundings. I don't know why, but his harmless, well-fed body reminded me of the life I had known in my own city.

Adler, on the other hand, was a creature who seemed hardly to have any real body at all.

Something weary, something primeval seemed to fill out the suit with the big checks that he always wore. He was by no means the smallest boy in the class. In fact he was about my build, for we stood next to each other in the gymnasium-period.

But he certainly had the biggest head among us all. His hair was bright red and fell over an incredibly high forehead, which had a peculiar habit of blotching with red whenever he was aroused in any way. Adler was extremely near-sighted and wore thick eye-glasses. The general expression of his features can best be described as a pathetic absentmindedness that would on occasion continue for half an hour at a time.

His vacant stare, however, would change suddenly into a frown like a thunder-cloud, and then into a grin, into a smile, coupled with some terse observation that used to affect me like an electric shock.

I tried myself in the office today and felt the same electric shock: that was how I recognized Adler. When he uttered the words, "The first time while I was still a student," I seemed to feel the impact of his personality on mine like a jet of flame. Strange, that until that moment I should have remembered nothing at all about him. Then I recalled his face, his voice, and his odd manner of speaking. This sudden evocation of an almost abysmal force, followed by an equally sudden subsidence, had not changed at all.

When I entered St. Nikolaus, Adler was considered one of the best students. Kio declared that he was lazy and never prepared his lessons properly; but his work was practically perfect, and his answers, though they were never given in the usual way, were correct. Adler had his own methods. In this he was the exact opposite of the prize pupil, Fischer, who was much less quick at grasping the content of his lessons than he was at remembering and echoing the singsong in which they were repeated in class.

Adler usually had difficulty in answering, and always spoke as though he had just been startled out of a deep sleep. What he said and the way he said it did not conform to the usual practice, so that Fischer and the pedants among the faculty were visibly annoyed whenever he spoke. In the school, as in all human relations, there existed what I may call a "conventional rhythm." The model pupil was he who possessed a good ear for this inner harmony and treated it with respect. It is the same thing in my office. I become annoyed if I find unaccustomed changes in the legal phraseology. Where may not such changes lead? We upholders of order must call a halt somewhere and guard ourselves against invasion by the innovator who has no reverence for form.

Kio, our teacher, while never approving Adler's originality, nevertheless had some understanding of it and was secretly sympathetic. In reprisal he called Adler "the philosopher," and liked to use the names Seneca and Descartes in calling on him in class. At the time I joined the class, Adler enjoyed the unquestioned respect of his fellow students. It had never occurred to any of them that there was something ridiculous about him. And at first even I fell under the influence of this universal respect. Only at times, when he was solemnly gazing into thin air, or when he jerked out his profound but muddled answers, I felt an inclination to giggle, though I quickly repressed it.

They were all agreed that this red-headed boy would become the great man through whose accomplishments the world would remember this class. When I say all, I mean, of course, an intellectual minority, though this minority gave the general tone to the whole class.

The great majority of the boys were interested principally in sports, and had organized a football-team. But the others had a way of treating these young athletes as an inferior caste. I still remember vividly what an impression of superiority I had when the group of intellectual boys—who happened also to be chiefly those who were well-to-do— bestowed on the young athletes the "soul of a football." The originator of this gift was Adler. After school-hours he usually wandered about alone or with one of his disciples. From the incident of the "soul of a football," however, it was obvious that he was a leader in spite of his solitariness.

As a newcomer, I had a hard time of it, at first, in this boyish society which spoke a different language from mine and had evolved from a different kind of childhood. Besides, their leaders possessed a degree of education that frequently left me in embarrassing situations.

I early betrayed the fact that I was a poor student, though this in itself would not have impaired my standing among my new comrades if I had been amusing or off-hand about it, or inventive in covering it up. But my answers were simply clumsy. A future as a nonentity was threatening me. A little more, and I should have sunk into the ranks of the athletes, or even the outcasts—to the lowest levels of the proletariat, where Komarek lurked—had not the memory of my father urged me on; while a conversation which I had with my classroom neighbor, Burda, changed the whole course of my life.

It was generally understood among the students that Adler was a highly-gifted poet and thinker, who wrote poetic dramas and essays on philosophy. The elect few who had read his works spoke of them with admiration, and only in whispers, as though they were some priceless secret.

One day Burda told me—perhaps to do me a favor, perhaps only to brag about his illustrious fellow student before a newcomer—at any rate, he told me that Adler had just completed a new dramatic work, which was to have its first reading shortly at Bland's house.

I received this information with a quiet indifference, while really burning with a hitherto unfelt ambition, and replied that Adler's drama interested me very much, especially since I wrote and had written so much myself.

This was not altogether a lie. I had written a few poems, but, not attaching much value to them, had refrained from showing them to anyone.

Burda, Adler's disciple, looked me over from head to foot.

"Aha!" he said. "So you write poetry!"

Then I really lied.

"The *Vienna Times* has printed a number of my poems in its Sunday supplement."

It was not a premeditated fraud; it was an inspired lie. At a single stroke I had become more than a boy admired by other boys. Serious men had published my work. I caught a glint in Burda's eyes that made my spirits soar. He, credulous soul, asked no proof of my boast. His class-patriotic heart was but too ready to acclaim me.

As we were leaving the classroom, after the noon-bell rang, Adler stopped me. It was the first fairly long talk between us. He gazed at me with his mobile eyes.

"So you are a poet."

A terrible smothering sensation spread over my body. At the same time I felt that I was going to leap at the boy's throat or burst out into hysterical laughter.

He continued to question me.

"I understand that you send your poems to the newspapers. Why do you do that?"

Like a coward, I embroidered my first lie.

"Of course, I don't use my own name. I use a pen-name."

But I could not quite mislead him.

"Why should you do that? Your poems certainly can't be mature work. . . . We're all too young yet for that."

It did not sound as if he meant to hurt my feelings. His last sentence was calculated to place me on a plane with him, and was spoken in a friendly way. But I wanted to weep. I wanted to shriek at the thought that this boy, with the large head and flashing eyes, was my superior. On him my lie had had no effect. Beside it he set his own innate sincerity, whose object was not personal success of any kind, but truth itself.

In my career as a student I had hitherto accepted all humiliations and failures lightly and carelessly. Now, for the first time, the consciousness of my own inferior position awoke in me. It was during the brief conversation with Adler, whose sincerity so reproached me, that I really found myself. My position now for the first time appeared intolerable to me. I was swept by a passion to excel and break this red-haired boy, whose manner so tormented me. Why should anyone stand above me? I can say with certainty that at that moment my father's character awoke in me.

The next day Bland and Burda solemnly invited me to attend the initial reading of Adler's work.

In the intellectual group in our class Bland played an important rôle. He was the son of a deputy and the possessor of a room that was separated from the rest of his father's house, so that it was particularly suitable for our gatherings. He was Adler's most intimate friend, and by far the most erudite of us all. He collected books, and we could always find Nietzsche, Mach, and all the latest poets at his house. Books were sacred to him. One could see it in the way he handled them. He never lent books, and we were compelled to read them in his room or not at all. He lived, and even loved, according to the rules he found in books. Later, when he fell in love with a married woman, he was completely upset by the serious problem which all

the books he had read made of the subject. His was an extraordinarily sensitive, an extraordinarily ethical nature. An
opponent of war, he joined the ranks and fell in battle. For
his inflexible moral sense commanded him to do so.

At four o'clock, after classes were over, we gathered in
Bland's room, which is still so vivid to me that I sometimes
see it in my dreams. I sat on the bed between Faltin and
Burda. Schulhof had thrown himself on the divan. Ressl,
the stout, kept changing his place continually. All places
were equally uncomfortable to him. I still see poor Bland
as he sat before his writing-table, overloaded with books.
Adler had backed his chair against the glass connecting-
door, for the light in the room was dim.

The hero of his tragedy was the famous Emperor Frederick II of Hohenstaufen, that Faustian free-thinker of the
Middle Ages, as Adler called him. The play made so profound an impression on me that whole stanzas of the con-
cluding scene still remain in my memory.

In the play, the Emperor is lying on his death-bed in his
palace in Sicily. The faithful are praying for his soul's
salvation, while he is uttering blasphemies directly to God.
They are awaiting the coming of the papal legate to save
the blasphemer's soul from Hell. The Pope's ambassador
arrives. He brings with him the sacrament to give to the
Emperor, provided the latter will recant his heresy. He
also brings a papal bull to damn the Emperor eternally if
he refuses to cease his defiance. The knights and ladies of
the court plead with the dying man not to refuse salvation.
In vain. Just as the embittered priest is about to pronounce
the damnation, Frederick raises his body in ecstasy and
whispers, "Ah, now, now, I see the truth . . . !" There is a

cry of satisfaction. All are hanging on the Emperor's lips, to catch the words of his confession through the death-rattle. The cardinal bends down and pronounces the Credo softly, so that the Emperor can repeat it after him. But Frederick, with his last remaining strength, thrusts away the legate and cries, "God is . . ." And in the middle of this sentence he falls back and dies. The eternal mystery, which he had solved in dying, remains unfathomed.

Even now, when I think of the handling of that scene, I am impressed. To be sure, it was the work of a sixteen-year-old boy, reminiscent, hyperbolic, and with serious gaps in experience. Yet it was from hearing Adler's tragedy that I first came to understand what is moving in all human works of art. Adler imagined human beings, directed their destinies, and did not botch them, but carried them through consistently to their ends. And his way of doing this, his way of reading his work, was so absorbed, so impersonal and so pure! Never for a moment did his glance stray to his audience. I seemed to see the elements of a higher type of beauty in his big head, with its red hair. An intellectual, a charismatic beauty played over his features while he was reading.

On that afternoon, if ever, I was prepared to forget my own ego and worship the superior qualities of one greater than I. I stood at those crossroads of which the poet spoke when he wrote, "Against another's superiority there is no salvation but love."

If only it had not been Franz Adler sitting opposite me, with his customary awkward pose, constantly peering into his note-book with his near-sighted eyes, even after he had finished reading.

Fascinated as I was, I again had difficulty in repressing my desire to laugh as I watched his shy, self-conscious gestures during the reading.

Schulhof was not satisfied with the monotonous way Adler read. He wanted to display his own craftsmanship and began to recite certain passages from the manuscript. He shouted and tried to make himself appear impressive.

But Bland quietly took the note-book out of his hand.

I was ready to admit that the battle, for me, was lost. It seemed as if my self-interest must have been effectually silenced. How could I ever hope to achieve anything like that? Any feeling of rivalry with such talent would be merely presumptuous. And yet—it is very hard to write nothing but the truth here—in my dark heart of hearts I was furious. It was no mere envy that I felt. I have never really been envious of anyone. Probably I would never have begrudged the laurel to anyone but Adler. And did I begrudge it even to him? Did I really hate him? I solemnly swear, at this time, that I have never for a single moment really hated Adler. But I could not endure his superiority, precisely because it was *his*.

Why? After all, belated explanations are never very satisfying. And I am constantly fighting with myself for accuracy. Was my repugnance really based on the fact that I was conscious of the Jew in Adler, that is, of the race from which the world is willing to accept everything but superiority?

After we had discussed the play and its characters for hours, we decided to meet in Bland's room the following day. I was to read some of my poems at that meeting.

Worried, and in a bad humor, I went home.

What was I going to do? I had written a few poems; but since I had heard Adler's tragedy, I hated them. They seemed utterly superficial and uninspired to me. I had let myself be tempted into a dangerous situation which could result only in my own shame and further triumph for the author of "Frederick II."

I read over the whole stupid sheaf of poems that lay in my desk—all the mixed metaphors, false emotions, and borrowed ideas that propped up my rhymes. Now I would have to reap the fruit of my boasting. I could not and would not withdraw now. But to recite my wretched poetry to the hypersensitive ears of Adler and his friends—it was impossible! Deciding quickly, I went into my aunts' library.

How remarkably easy I found lies and deceit at that time. I cannot recall that I was deterred by the slightest scruple. Was I perverse? And if so, how different from my father! He was a judge, every inch of him. Cold and hard as he was, unswerving justice was frozen in his heart. But I have no sense of justice. That is why I am really not a judge at all. I am too much of a coward ever to be a good judge. They think I am mad to refuse promotion to the supreme court. They are mistaken, for it is something very profound in my nature that makes me refuse. I have no right to be a judge and hand down decisions; I must live and die an examining magistrate.

After a brief search in the library, I found a book that seemed to answer my purposes. It was the poetic works of a forgotten Revolutionary poet of the 1848 period, an aged volume, of which there was not likely to be another copy in existence.

The poet's name was Justus Frey. I have not forgotten that name.

Without stopping to do much selecting, I copied out two poems with a stanza-form that was fluent and musical. One of them was entitled, "What Is It You Call Great?"

It seemed to be directed against Napoleon and the military-hero cult in general. But it was not its pacifist tenor, with which I have never had much sympathy, but its melodiousness, that pleased me. The poem also had a persuasive quality in it, somewhat similar to that suggested by Adler's "Frederick." Of all the stanzas, only one has stayed in my mind.

"What is it you call great?
The hero's head with murder for a crown,
Whose armed heel stamps the wind-blown harvests down,
That send out of the earth their golden weight,—
This you call great?"

This poem, which I recited without the slightest shyness, had an immediate effect on Schulhof, Faltin, and Ressl. Schulhof immediately learned a few stanzas by heart. Bland was quite moved and said, "It sounds as though it had not been written in our time."

Even Adler praised it with a few words of admiration.

"You have a very musical diction," he said. "Perhaps it is because you are Viennese."

He seemed never to have given me a thought before, for he was now visibly racking his brains for words in praise of my talent. After a while he turned to me and said: "Tell me, what do these things that you have written about

—war and Napoleon—mean to you? I should never have thought they'd interest you very much. . . ."

Was this more of that presumption that I was always imagining I saw in him? No, I believe it was a profound and exquisite sensitivity to outraged truth. Certainly Adler never doubted the genuineness of the poems, and yet he had a feeling that something about them was not quite right. Again he made me feel how far above me he towered—this homely boy with the incorruptible soul. The consciousness of my own deceit clutched at my throat.

Yet by means of this little plagiarism I had won a place of respect for myself among my comrades. Their attitude toward me changed completely. Now when I gave ridiculous answers to questions in class and talked rank nonsense, it was justified as the natural distraction of a poetic mind.

So that I owe it to this dishonorable affair that my reputation rose. I began to feel at ease again.

The two women with whom I lived allowed me every sort of liberty. For example, I could go to the theatre any night I chose; and I made unlimited use of this privilege. The habit of theatre-going, which still drives me to waste so many nights, is a product of that time. For I have only a moderate interest in actors or singers, in comedies or opera. The stage itself bores me a good deal. But the excitement of the audiences, the murmur of crowds, the fleeting charm of the women, the promenade between the acts—all these things have the same powerful attraction for me now as when I was a boy and life still seemed hopelessly beyond my reach. A year ago, this murmur of life affected me with unusual force in the foyer of a little theatre in Paris; and I had to leave the house hurriedly, for the exhilaration I felt was bitter with remorse. . . .

Schulhof, Faltin, and I used to go early to the box-office. This was part of our strategy for securing a good place in the gallery or among the standees.

At the theatre Faltin was in his element. Not only had he seen every play and heard every opera in the course of his short life, but he also knew to a dot the lives of all the actors and the gossip of the dressing-rooms. Although his parents were poor and he himself possessed no musical gifts of any kind, he wheedled permission from them to make a pilgrimage to Bayreuth during the summer. He was instinctively drawn to the centre of events. In our local theatre he knew by name all the ladies who sat in the loges. In spite of his defective hearing, he would insist that the tenor was singing off-key or that the soprano's rendition was "glassy."

Schulhof, on the other hand, imitated all the actors, and could recite from memory whole passages out of the dryest French comedies. I can still see him standing in the corridor outside our classroom, a watch-crystal screwed into his eye, bowing sarcastically to Faltin and saying: "Make haste, my dear Marquis. Try your luck! Who knows whether later on Madame de Blainville may be in a position to receive you. . . ."

Our theatre-going gave me the idea of starting a dramatic club in our class, a reading-circle in which each one of us would assume different rôles from the great dramas of literature.

The same idea springs up in the sixth form of every

academy in the country. But in this case, it was I, the stranger at St. Nikolaus, who first thought of it.

Burda immediately took up the idea and questioned Adler about it. Adler ordered us to meet at Bland's house. There Adler, Bland, Schulhof, Faltin, Ressl, and I founded the dramatic society. We excitedly discussed the ends and aims of our organization and laid down strict rules for the conduct of meetings.

Adler, however, remained surprisingly indifferent. But I was radiant. Yes, now I felt my power. At last I was naturalized at St. Nikolaus. The despised intruder had turned out to be a more than useful member of the class. How I loved that reading-circle! Two or three times a year it would bring out some notable production. Then we would invite the whole class, the astonished football-team, perhaps even the other classes, and so, within a short time, have all St. Nikolaus Academy at our feet. Perhaps in the fullness of my triumph I said too much for my own good that afternoon; for Adler remained cold to the project.

On the way home, I walked alone with him, along the same streets that I still traverse daily on my way to the courthouse. With mounting enthusiasm I kept developing new details of our society, suggested "The Robbers" as the first work for presentation, and even assigned the parts, reserving the rôle of Franz Moor for myself.

Then Adler stopped short. It was a dull-gray winter evening. He was wearing a thin coat and seemed to be freezing. His face was pale. Perhaps he did not consider what he was saying. He drew himself up to his full height and said: "What is your idea, anyway? You presume a good deal for your size. You ought to be glad that we let you take part at all, and should wait till your own rôle is given you."

With such words a leader might have rebuked the arrogance of some follower who was reaching too eagerly for his power.

These words were destined to prove Adler's greatest sin in this world. They were more. They were his fate; for they let loose a devil in me. It may sound foolish, but I believe, and this belief burns in me even now like a scorching fire, that if Adler had never uttered that one sentence, he would not have been standing before me today, a ruined man.

I could not answer a single word. I simply turned and fled. My eyes were quite red when I came down to supper; and my aunts were much disturbed at my appearance. Adler's unjustified attack had struck home. The reading-circle had been my one creation, my first successful attempt to take root in a strange soil. Previously I had even thought of changing schools in the middle of the year.

That night I suffered from an attack of such desolating, racking passion as I had never known in my life before. I think it must have been desire for revenge that I felt; for I am by nature vindictive. In the morning I was calm again, but tired. My wounded pride was still smarting.

I immediately informed Burda of my resignation from the newly-formed reading-circle.

My position among my classmates was already so well-established that the resignation made a strong impression and won me new respect. The boys begged me insistently to retract my decision, but I remained adamant. It was not difficult for me to refuse to play a rôle among them, since I had known them only for a month of so. In the meanwhile, I hinted, they need have no qualms about accepting my idea and my plan of organization, which really was mine and no one's else.

Nothing happened for several days except that Burda, Adler, and Bland were continually putting their heads together rather openly. At the beginning of the next week, however, Burda came to my house and proposed that I should become secretary of our society. Naturally Adler would have to be president. It was clear that Bland had refused this honor, which he was by far the best fitted to exercise, in order to conciliate and win me back to them. This meant a great deal; it was a high honor and a real triumph for me! I no longer refused.

Then the reading-circle became an established institution. We met twice a week, and no longer exclusively in Bland's room. Every member in turn permitted us the use of his room whenever he was able. We began, as I had proposed, with the "The Robbers." No one tried to take the part of Franz from me, while Schulhof would not give up that of the youthful hero, Karl. We did not sit around a table, but went noisily through our gestures, book in hand. Adler declared he was content to take all the smaller rôles in the piece. Ressl was particularly good at playing women's parts, because his hair was blond and he had fair skin and was stout.

I built up my poetic reputation artfully. Before we took up Schiller, I was often reading poems with the best of them. Justus Frey proved an inexhaustible source of inspiration. Adler himself was rather apathetic at the meetings. Perhaps our actions were really distasteful to him. He looked like a person who was undergoing some physical change. I tried to avoid being alone with him.

How long and how full the days of boyhood are!

As my own days grew longer and fuller, I thought I had forgotten how deeply Adler had wounded me. In reality, I merely no longer thought about it. But his insulting words were smouldering deep in my nature. They had grown to be an ugly feeling that was trying to force its way into the light of day, and which did finally break loose in a totally unexpected manner. I am much the same today as I was then—resentful without being aware of it. Suddenly something will spring up, which may have been smouldering for years in my own inner darkness, but which takes me completely by surprise. If I were not resentful, would I still resent this incident even today?

Weeks slid by.

As I have already said, Adler was my neighbor in our gymnasium-class. In Vienna I had earned a good reputation as a gymnast. But at St. Nikolaus, where there were so many intellectuals and bookworms, I had got somewhat out of my old habits. The over-emphasis placed on mentality by one section of my fellow students, together with their contempt for all physical exercise, explains why no one paid much attention to Adler in this class. His enormous head, with its thick glasses, his scrawny neck, his stiff-jointed legs and lifeless body (we exercised in our shirts) were no sight to gladden the eye of an athlete. But no one had ever paid any attention to Adler's physique, though it was certainly an obstacle to any kind of bodily activity. At least such was the impression made on me by the body of this talented intellectual. Even the martinet gymnasium-instructor accepted Adler's physique without a word. What could he do? Adler was Adler.

One day (we were then in the second semester) we were practising an exercise called "the scissors," on the parallel bars. It is a simple trick that any child can do with a little skill. In mid-circle you turn around and end up astride the bar.

I had finished my "scissors" with a splendid swing. Then came Adler's turn. Slowly, with his legs sagging at the knees, he walked up to the apparatus. His heavy mind was lost in thought, and he presented a strange appearance. Everyone gazed at him in a kind of trance. He pulled himself up on the bar with some effort, and there he stuck. Then he shut his eyes, and that solemn stare began to overspread his face. His mouth fell open; and, while the upper part of his body hung stiff and helpless, his legs began to swing in an indescribable way, as though on hinges.

Still everyone remained serious. Even I could have controlled my desire to laugh, as I had so often done before. But suddenly my resentment came over me with a rush, for I saw my superior in all his pitiableness. And this time, this time, I did not want to control myself. A peal of laughter, like the devil's own, burst from my throat.

At first all the students looked at me in amazement. But then the players on the football-team, themselves all good athletes, one after another began to join in my guffaws, tentatively at first, but gradually growing louder and more scornful. Vengeance against Adler's mind was smouldering in their hearts, too. The diabolic quality in my laughter was so infectious that suddenly everyone burst out in merriment. Even Bland could not refrain. As I remember it, only Komarek, that savage youth, remained unmoved.

At last our gymnasium-instructor, whose whole face was lit up with a malicious grin, said, "To tell the truth, Adler, nobody could look at you now and keep from smiling."

These words brought on another peal of that hysterically cruel laughter, that bitingly contemptuous laughter, of which only a class of schoolboys is capable.

"Have another try at it, Adler," our instructor commanded, giving free rein to a long-pent-up dislike. And Adler, amidst louder and louder salvos of guffaws, sat swinging his legs helplessly. He made a few desperate movements, rocked to and fro on the bars, and at last, as the instructor did not come to his rescue as usual, dropped to the mat exhausted.

When he got back to his place in line, the laughter had died out, but everyone turned away from him as though embarrassed. No one said a word. At last the class came to an end.

We had dressed in the locker-room of the gymnasium and were leaving the schoolhouse, when Adler beckoned to me. There were big red blotches on his forehead.

"You ought to be ashamed of yourself," he said.

"Why should I be ashamed? Because you happen to be a bungler?"

He came up close to me. His eyes were shut tight. Then we began to wrestle. It was a long and fierce struggle. All the wounds of my old humiliation broke open in the course of it and gave me new strength. I had need of it, too, for Adler displayed a savage and surprising power. On the parallel bars, he had given up. But now, with all the others looking on, he knew what was at stake. How much I had underestimated his strength! His muscles and sinews tightened. Rage taught him adroitness and where to grip.

Adler constricted my chest until I was breathless. More than once I thought I was lost. Never will I be able to forget that terrible, silent struggle. We were wrestling for our very lives. Woe to me, if Adler vanquished me physically, too. No one offered to part us. Everyone seemed to understand that this was no ordinary boyish tussle, but a life-and-death struggle. The circle of spectators stood watching in deadly silence.

Then I felt that my heart could not stand the strain any longer. Perspiration was soaking my shirt. I was growing weak, while Adler's forehead was still dry. He wrestled without exertion, his strength seeming to come from some profound reserve. Only our quick, hoarse panting broke the silence.

Then he encircled my neck and began to choke me. As he did so, I found that I had the underhold, and I threw him to the ground with all the strength of my rage. He tried to rise to his feet again, but I, flooded with some kind of indescribable joy, forced back his shoulders and knelt on his chest. Then I arose—the victor.

But Adler lay still for a long time with his eyes shut before he arose. Nobody said a word. Most of them tried to act as though there had been no enmity involved and it had been simply a good-natured wrestling-bout.

I offered Adler my hand in all sincerity. He took it, and we left each other with a murmured "Good night." At that moment I felt as if I really loved him.

On the way home I ran into Komarek. He took his

hands out of his pockets long enough to say, "I saw from
the first that you were a common sort. . . ."

I heard this insult well enough, but paid no attention to
it, and went along, whistling.

Next morning, in the Homer class, Adler for the first
time did not know the answer. He simply did not open
his mouth when called on to translate. Kio walked silently
to and fro, once or twice, growling, "What's the matter with
you, Adler? Are you sick or haven't you had enough
sleep?" But he was considerate and called on someone else.

That afternoon I walked home from school with Adler.
For the first time a profound philosophic conversation between us seemed to bind us together. We had come much
closer to each other.

Something had been decided. . . .

CHAPTER IV

WHAT was it that had been decided? What had happened? It is only now that I know the true answer. A work of annihilation had begun. It had begun with my laugh, with the wrestling-bout in which I had come off victor. It was to end twenty-five years later in the detention-cell of a prison. Truly, a slow, a mysterious process of annihilation, which I myself scarcely suspected, and which I surely could not control.

Though a hundred voices of reason within me make me doubt that things are as they really are, I feel as though some pressure on my breast were forcing me to write. I see that my hand has already covered six pages with rapid shorthand notes! Of course, it's absurd!

I am not even sure that my flying pen is really writing on the paper the details that my memory recalls.

It is three o'clock in the morning and I am not even tired. I feel fresher than I usually do, and wonderfully oblivious of external things. This feeling of obliviousness staggers me. As a rule, it takes me a full hour to write an average letter. But now a whole procession of strange, disembodied symbols is prancing before my eyes. Yes, the procession is prancing before me as though it were marching to some kind of feathery and soundless music.

Three o'clock in the morning! It is Sunday already. A long, long Sunday. . .

•   •   •   •   •

Soon it was easy to see what had happened. The change in my attitude was not gradual. Since I had laughed at him, since we had wrestled together, I myself no longer wanted to laugh at him. Quite the contrary. I sought his confidence. He had given up his superior attitude towards me. But, though I no longer laughed, others did. It commenced again in the next gymnasium-period, when Adler had to turn around the parallel bars. From the gymnasium it spread to the classrooms.

That laugh of mine had sown itself like seed, and was sprouting out of more than one throat by now. And this infectious mockery was destined to destroy all that authority to which Adler had bent even the uncouth gymnasium-instructor himself. It had already destroyed the respect that we commonly pay to an outstanding mentality and had put an end to the good-will which boys sometimes bestow even on one who is physically inept.

The members of the athletic club, on whom Adler had once bestowed a "soul," seized this opportunity to ridicule him. In triumph, they cast off the alien yoke of his intelligence. Even Ressl, Schulhof, and Faltin grew uncertain of their idol—even Burda—all of them, perhaps, with the exception of Bland. A few weeks' time had sufficed to change completely the relations of the entire class to Adler.

The old admiration which his disciples felt for him had not yet vanished, of course; but it was tinctured with a certain amount of good-natured amusement. The ridiculous traits in this gifted boy were now as clear as daylight to everyone; and, indeed, everyone was quite convinced that they always had been. But it was not only his physical awkwardness that had suddenly made his life a burden to him; even those profound and ponderous answers, which had once added not a little to his fame, now began to be laughed at in turn.

Is it not written somewhere in the Bible that "Whosoever shall say to his brother, 'Thou fool,' shall suffer hell-fires?"

Yet the words, "You fool," were becoming ever more frequent in the sixth form at St. Nikolaus Academy.

It is true that I did not laugh now. But Schulhof, Ressl, and the others did, whenever Kio, with a sudden question, would startle Adler out of his solemn day-dreams, while, stammering awkwardly, he strove to clothe his ideas in words. Kio, too, seemed to have become infected by the new influence. Previously he had always groped for the sense of what Adler was saying and translated it in his own words. But now, bewildered and angry at the laughter of the students, he would shout at Adler: "What sort of rigmarole are you laboring over now? I take it as a personal affront." And the laughter would simply grow louder, feeding on Kio's comicalities. If Adler had made any resistance at that time, if he had shielded himself against our laughter, if, in those crucial days, he had taken a firm grip on his reins and secretly studied and shown up the teacher in front of the class, no doubt he could have saved himself. But he allowed them to make a guy of him without so much as lifting a hand against it. Never in all my life have I seen a more defenseless soul than Adler. It was not merely that he made no resistance to the gathering storm of ridicule. The most terrible part was yet to come.

For, one day, after stammering out some confused mysti-

cal answer until Kio told him to sit down, Adler himself
burst out laughing. It was terrifying; the effect of it on us
can never be described. His face became a flaming red, his
eyes flashed, and his lips kept moving as though at last they
had found the word they were groping for, but could not
utter it. He had made a bow to the teacher and stumbled
blindly to his seat. It was when he heard the soft titter that
received him that he himself suddenly broke into a guffaw.

There was more than self-ridicule in it—there was self-
annihilation. It was my laugh echoed, the laugh with
which I had ruined him. My vengeful laughter had stuck
quivering in his soul, like the sharp barb of a poisoned
arrow. The memory of my infectious laughter had been
destroying him from that hour on. It was not only his
classmates who were destroying him; Adler was destroying
himself.

As long as he had had faith in his friends, he had felt
strong and proud. But now that that faith had succumbed
to the first onslaught, were all his forces going to crumble
to nothing? What was the cause of this? Did the strength
of the mind that had composed "Frederick" really de-
pend on the support of boys, his inferiors? Did their outer
repudiation of him liberate in him that inner sense of fu-
tility which is the curse of all intellectuals? These are idle
speculations. But it was a strange disintegration. I still do
not understand it; though Adler's laugh ought to be familiar
enough to doctors and lawyers.

Presently the downfall began in earnest. One by one the
teachers withdrew their favor from him. Kio's greatest
weakness was his painful distrust of people. As Adler's
answers always brought laughter now, Kio began to imagine

that the unfortunate boy was clowning for the amusement of the class. And "a personal affront" was the thing that he forgave least in this world. I think that only the history-teacher remained friendly to Adler to the end. It was not a result of my seeking, but rather my fate, that as Adler began to descend, I myself rose in the scales. At that time I was generally considered negligent but bright.

With the help of Justus Frey, my reputation began to grow in the dramatic club, from day to day. Pretty soon I even ventured to smuggle in some of my own poems under the ægis of my plagiarisms. My credit was so well-established that nobody noticed the difference. I had become the leading figure in our circle, and Burda began to enthuse over me as he had previously over Adler.

Meanwhile Adler and the class seemed to adjust themselves with surprising quickness to their changed relationship. Soon no one even troubled to remember that things had once been otherwise. The members of our society were drawn closer to one another. Of course, Adler was still with us, though no longer as *primus inter pares*. We were all of us too constantly together to observe clearly the change that had taken place in him. It would be absurd to suppose that this change was the result of my handiwork alone. The workings of his own nature had already prepared the ground. But it was certainly I who, in the decisive hour, had intervened in his fate. Had it not been for me, Adler might have been a . . . Nonsense!

The end of the semester and of the school-year was at hand. Adler and I received report-cards that looked as like as two peas. But my marks were a good deal better than his, for he had slipped back in several subjects.

During the distribution of report-cards and the brief summary which Kio was in the habit of making at the close of the school-year, he turned to Adler.

"What have you been up to in these last few months, Adler?" he asked. "The faculty can't recognize you any longer for the same boy. You'd better make an effort to pull yourself together during vacation. Take a warning from me: I see Nemesis looming behind you."

He used those exact words. I can swear to it with a clear conscience; for everything now seems alive to me again in memory.

After a few weeks, which completely washed away all recollection of the causes of Adler's downfall, we found ourselves together again at St. Nikolaus. Only, now we were seventeen. The longest and the most decisive year of my life had begun.

I had arrived at what then seemed more than likely would be my destiny. In the course of time I have learned to control my instincts somewhat. "But the ram shall be driven into the wilderness." *Agnus dei, qui tollit peccata mundi!*

It was I who introduced "playing hookey" into the seventh form at St. Nikolaus Academy.

We did not cut classes because of any fear of examinations or to escape the monotony of school-work, but from a suddenly awakened impulse to break through the established order of the world. While "Fischer, Robert" was droning out his knowledge in regulation singsong, while "Komarek, August" was enduring the abuses of his teachers, while the dullards, heedless and deedless, were momentarily growing duller over their books, it was now my habit to wander freely, though perilously, through the outlying quarters of the city, and to loiter in cafés, awaiting what adventures life might send.

It was (I cannot stress this too much), it was a criminal impulse that possessed me. In the previous year, during the first months of my sojourn at St. Nikolaus, I had observed the effect that genius has on people. If I had not succeeded in destroying this effect, through the hateful power which arose within me at that time, I should have had nothing to resist it with, for I myself am merely an ordinary mortal. Simply in order to save myself, I, too, was driven to invent something new. If it could not be done on the highest plane (plagiarism always remained plagiarism to me) I was content to let it be on the lowest.

As a starter, I seduced Ressl and Schulhof. Later Faltin joined us, then Adler. As circumstances favored, others were also recruited from time to time. As, in the previous year, I had organized the reading-circle, I now drew up some prudent rules for playing hookey. For every class a boy cut he was supposed to bring a duly-signed excuse from home. It was no great difficulty for me to forge my good Aunt Aurelia's name. And I very cleverly forged similar excuses for the others also. Soon I could imitate the signatures of a number of parents, with a single flourish of my hand. I made further arrangements to have Burda meet us clandestinely after school at various previously determined spots about the city (preferably houses with a back and a front entrance), in order to inform us what had taken place in class, whether any of the teachers were suspicious or whether everything was calm. Burda was our secret agent. He did not dare play hookey himself, but he considered us heroes because of our boldness. His gentle face would be quite pale and terrified as he came to seek us outlaws. This enhanced the romantic daring of those long days.

We would come together at eight o'clock in the morning at some remote spot, which, as part of the game, we reached by a series of detours, using the most roundabout street-car lines. We would wander excitedly through the suburbs, enter some dingy café, reeking of stale beer, that seemed villainous enough for us, and there play billiards, drink whiskey, and talk about the decay of the world. The decadent literature of the period with which Bland had made us familiar may have had some share in shaping the manner of our excesses. I still recall the hellish pride with which I would utter the words, "Children, we are undone. . . ."

In this way I daily proved to my schoolmates that I was a leader of a truly remarkable kind.

I no longer remember precisely at what moment I first felt stirring within me that voluptuous cruelty which kept driving me to torment Adler. I think it began with our drinking.

Wine comes to me as a release, as it does to all people who are serious by nature. It stimulates and exalts me. On Adler, on the other hand, alcohol had just the opposite effect; and at first he seemed profoundly nauseated by it. At such times I would observe that a student who could not drain off his tumbler of whiskey at one gulp would play a sorry rôle at the university. Then I would pass Adler another glass. Ressl, always personally affronted if anyone declined enjoyment of any sort, would back me up. At first Adler used to fall asleep after the second glass. We would wake him and make him empty a third, and then a fourth glass. At this point he would pass into a delirious, almost idiotic condition. He would reel around the café, shaking his fist in the faces of invisible opponents, his own features distorted in an expression of pain. I used to watch him, fascinated. At last, I thought, his anger must break out again! Surely he would hurl himself on me again! It was a kind of desire in me. But Adler never even cast a glance at me. He would simply dance around and stammer plaintive words, appeals and weird poetry such as I have never heard from any other human soul. At the end of his dance he would frequently fall to the floor. Then we would roll around in our seats with laughter, and Adler would laugh with us. From the confines of consciousness he would still peal out that convulsive, self-destructive laugh.

But after about two weeks he began slowly to accustom himself to sweet liqueurs. At the same time, one unusually strong appetite began to develop in Adler, the only one I ever observed in him—a sweet tooth. In the afternoons we used to gather at a confectioner's which Ressl had discovered in the inner city. Ressl's pockets were always well-lined with money. I, too, had nothing to complain about in this respect; for my doting aunts used to slip me a few silver coins every day, and on Sundays a bank-note, although my father had ordained a Spartan allowance of pocket-money.

Adler never had any money. In the days before we were "undone," as long as he and his mind had prevailed, his pennilessness had never struck anyone as odd. But now the reading of one's own poetry, and even the dramatic club, had lost favor. "Life" (as at that time I used to call our peregrinations) was in the ascendant. But for "life" one needed money.

Adler was the son of an invalid widow without means. He never mentioned her in conversation. In fact, he never said a word about himself or any of the circumstances of his intimate life. Adler's father had committed suicide years before, and the boy had been brought up under the stern hand of a very disagreeable old guardian. This person, his uncle, owned a dry-goods store on one of the principal thoroughfares of a growing suburb. And the storekeeper was irritably waiting to take on the author of "Frederick of Hohenstaufen, a Tragedy of Faith" as a clerk without wages. Adler knew that at the slightest sign of slackening in his studies, his guardian would take him out of school and hurl him into the hated abyss of business. He seemed to live in considerable dread of his uncle and not to get along very well with his mother, so that he never liked to ask either of them for money.

But when Adler stood in front of the confectioner's showcase, and the aroma of chocolate, cream, glacé fruit, and puff-paste assailed his nostrils, a kind of morbid greed seemed to overpower him, something uncontrollable and strikingly out of keeping with his reserved nature. His hands would twitch and his lips quiver. Above all other pastry he adored tarts. Ressl and I used to pay for the quantities he consumed. He seemed to take our liberality for granted, until one day Ressl said, "Now that I stop to think of it, Adler, I don't exactly know why I should have to stand for your insatiable appetite for fruit-tarts every day. . . ."

Adler drew back his hand and the fork that he was in the act of extending for a sweetmeat.

Ressl goaded him further.

"Sebastian," he said, "did you ever hear of such a thing? Why should the two of us have to pay for him? What return is he going to make us?"

I imitated his tone of voice:

"Oh, I suppose some day we'll be proud to think that Adler let us buy his fruit-tarts for him."

Ressl was delighted.

"An eye for an eye and a tooth for a tooth," he said. "He's got to make some return. Don't you agree with me, Sebastian?"

"Yes, I guess you can't get around that. He's got to make some return."

Adler pushed the empty plate away from him and stared at us in astonishment. Ressl kept up his deadly serious air.

"What sort of return do you suggest, Sebastian?" he asked.

Without stopping to consider, as if my reply had not come from my own brain but had been whispered in my ear, I said quickly, "Buy him a tart, Ressl, and let him kneel before you if he wants it."

Ressl is a person absolutely devoid of fine feelings.

"You're a hard bargainer, Sebastian," he said, delighted. "But one tart isn't payment enough. Get down on your knees, Adler, and I'll buy you three fruit-tarts."

Adler stared at us, as though in amazement, for a long time; then he slowly pushed away his plate, and with his stiff gait left the store.

Another day I managed things so that Adler and I entered the confectioner's alone toward evening. There was no one in the shop but the proprietor. In silence I consumed two whole fruit-tarts, although I could hardly cram them down from excitement and disgust. In silence, too, Adler stood behind and watched me. I waited a little while longer and then I turned to him.

"Would you like one?"

He took a fork and a plate from the counter. My courage had left me, but his sudden movement made my baseness somehow easier for me.

"Very well," I said, "but first kneel down." And suddenly what I had never expected, what I had never really wanted, happened. Adler raised his plate like a sacrificial salver high above his head and knelt down. The proprietor's eyes grew big with astonishment, though Adler was not kneeling before me, but facing the wall, where there were rows of little chocolate figures in the showcases. I quickly laid a tart on his plate. He rose and began to eat it. But after the second bite he stopped chewing, sank into thought, and finally pushed his plate away.

I paid, making a forced joke to give the incident the appearance of a schoolboy prank. I left the humiliated boy as quickly as possible. But as soon as I was alone I grew anxious. Ought I to run after him and beg his forgiveness? No, the crowds of people were carrying me onward. But I hated myself. Oh, how I hated myself! In this mood I swore for the future to control my impulse to torture Adler.

But things turned out otherwise.

Ressl had an elder brother, a sculptor, who lived in Munich. The stories that Fritz Ressl told us about this æsthetic young man called forth our most lively admiration.

He possessed, if his younger brother was not bragging, a marvellous studio filled with the most wonderful treasures, a famous collection of old oriental lamps which at night flooded the room with their magic glow. As if this were not enough, an organ was built into one wall of the studio. Ewald Ressl declared himself a believer in the mysterious forces of the universe.

At Christmas he visited his parents and accidentally spread a dangerous infection among us or at least what in the course of our mad boyish antics amounted to an infection. Ewald Ressl met us in his brother's room, and, as soon as he saw Adler, declared: "I see something lurking behind that boy. I see a green-and-violet sprite hovering near his head. He'd probably make a good medium."

He initiated us at once into the A-B-C of spiritualism and table-rapping. And lo and behold, when Adler sat in the magic circle, the ouija-board really did behave in a very strange way. It grew nervous. It seemed to be contemplating flight and tried to jump off the table.

Tonight I saw Ressl, Schulhof, and Faltin again, creatures with nothing at all ahead of them, and with nothing in the past, two-legged, God-created lumps of indifference like myself. Who would ever imagine that they are the same creatures inhabiting the same bodies as those boys in the past, driven to the verge of insanity by alcohol and mystical nonsense.

We held séances nearly every night. Perhaps the maddest part of our antics consisted in the fact that while we all believed in spirits, we suspected one another of moving the board. As for me, I knew that in critical moments, if not in general, I assisted the spirit in the ouija by mingling my own thoughts with its words. I was not sure about the others, and they admitted as little as I. Besides, we wanted to believe in the existence of spirits. To our minds the occult world was something wasted, disordered, "undone," a world the exact opposite of our middle-class lives. Those errant spirits with whom one sometimes succeeded in communicating were the Bohemia of the Beyond.

Parents, guardians, aunts might ridicule our belief in spirits or try to put us right, like Aunt Aurelia, who declared that spiritualism was a godless business; still our hearts used to pound during the séances as though they would jump out of our breasts. Cold terror lurked for us in the shadow of every darkened window or article of furniture. With aching heads and tingling spinal columns we would draw close together to discuss the teaching of Du Prel or Aksakov's animistic theory of the freedom of motion in intelligences still sojourning on earth. Then we would hear light taps on the wall of the next room. With a cry we would seek shelter in one another's arms.

We kept conjuring up the dead again and again, however, and strove to cultivate friendly relations with these newly-won and shady boon-companions of our spiritual anarchy. Even though I know that I myself never let slip a good opportunity to help along the spirits, so many incredible and fantastic things happened that even today I hesitate to ascribe all of them to the inventive genius of my fellow students.

As for Adler, I am willing to bet my life that he never cheated once.

The farther the year advanced, the more Adler, encouraged by us, accustomed himself to drinking; and the deeper we were plunged in our spiritualistic obsession, the sadder and more reticent the boy became. This sense of sadness served him as a kind of insulation.

We accepted Ewald Ressl's prediction that Adler was possessed of mediumistic powers. Now I do not believe that he possessed any such peculiar powers. But, at that time, I used to like to declare that he was a medium, probably simply because the idea of a medium implies something passive, feminine, and ambiguous. Now I understand very clearly motives which, at that time, I myself did not suspect.

But, if Adler was a medium, it was up to me to turn hypnotist. I must always be asserting my superiority over him; so I volunteered to throw him into a trance in the presence of the others. He objected and tried to get up and go away. But Schulhof forced him to come back and held him in the easy-chair. Then we made him take off his glasses. I stood in front of him, staring straight at him and striving to focus all the powers of my will on him. For the first time I looked into the depths of his eyes. His glasses were off, and the reddened eyelids were lifted. There were quiet, untroubled depths in those gray eyes. As I gazed into them I realized that Adler's opinion of me had never changed—never would change. The calmness of those pupils showed me that all my actions had never made him hate or even despise me. While, six feet away, I gazed at him as though insane, he simply looked me over quietly. I tried to intensify my efforts; I seized his hands and held my breath. Then he closed his eyes. He closed them with an expression of disgust. His head began to wobble, while half-stifled grunts came from his chest. But I also began to feel numbed. Adler's broad, red face seemed drawing closer and closer to mine; it seemed to turn into the sad round disc of the moon; it changed into a strange, illumined planet, floating alone in space. Perhaps I was merely an unfortunate star myself. But God had blessed Adler and not me. I was aware of it even at that moment, as at every other. Suddenly Adler thrust me aside, sprang up and ran out of the room. He had had to give in.

We carried on most of our antics in a big hall-like room in Ressl's house. Sometimes we would be at them until two or three o'clock in the morning.

It may be that not all the communications we held with spirits, during those manifestations which we thought we had induced, were just imagination or deceit on the part of one or another of us. Even if there was nothing truly supernatural in our séances, perhaps there was some trace, some atom of a troubled reality in them, which was not due to any deception of ours, but which hovered bewildered over our frightened circle. For our séances were a tangled confusion of deception, of desire to believe in spirits, of intoxication, of cynicism, and a number of other things. We always drank a great deal during these sittings.

Once, about four o'clock in the morning, an old woman in a white bath-robe and night-dress suddenly entered the room. It was Ressl's grandmother, the "old woman," as we used to call her. Long ago, she had sent her son, the great textile-manufacturer, Ressl, as a poor clerk into the great world. Now, shaking her head dubiously, she took care of the rich man's palace.

The first thing the old woman stared at was the fragments of expensive wine-glasses scattered all over the polished floor in little puddles of liquor. She stepped out of the shadow of the doorway and set about mopping up the floor with her handkerchief.

"Liquor-stains," she whined in a high voice. "You can't rub them off. Nothing will rub them off. What a shame!"

Then she began to scold us.

"You good-for-nothings, it's all your parents' fault. They do nothing but stuff you full of food. If you had to work for your living, you wouldn't be so free and easy with everything. You might have a chance then to grow up to be real men, too." She sat herself down among us.

"Go along now," she went on. "I won't get out of this chair till every last one of you is out of the house."

Ressl laughed and patted the angry old lady on the shoulder.

"The old woman's all right," he said, to reassure us. "She'd never peach."

Grumbling, she mimicked her impudent grandson. "The 'old woman,' the 'old woman' . . ." she said.

But we kept right on going to Ressl's and befuddling our wits with forbidden mysteries until late into the night.

One night, however, our madness reached a climax. There were four of us bearing the brunt of the séance— Ressl, Schulhof, Adler, and I. Faltin and Burda were keeping the record. Even Bland was present, though he remained sceptical in the face of the most stirring supernatural manifestations.

The ouija went hopping and clattering around the table so fast and with such big jumps that we could scarcely follow it.

Schulhof was leading the séance. In a solemn voice, he asked: "Is there a spirit present in the table? Rap if you want to answer. Once for 'yes' and twice for 'no.' Three times if you mean, 'I don't know.' "

The ouija trembled and tipped towards Adler. There was one loud knock: "Yes."

"Are you a man or a woman?" Schulhof demanded. "Rap once if you are a man, twice if you are a woman."

Two feeble taps followed.

"A woman," we whispered.

"Do you come from the dead?" asked Schulhof. "Answer."

A long pause followed, then there came three tremulous taps: "I don't know."

We looked at one another. "Perhaps she's dying at this moment," Ressl said.

A loud, and at the same time grateful "yes" rang out.

Schulhof's deep voice trembled as he asked: "Where are you now? Answer with the letters of the alphabet; one tap for A, two taps for B, three for C, and so on."

Straining our ears to hear, we bent over the constantly tilting ouija, as we feverishly pieced the letters together. The answer was, "On the border-line. . . ."

The words seemed like an icy hand touching us. The game went on.

"Name the place where you are!"

"The railroad-station!"

"Where is this station?"

The ouija hesitated, as though some countervailing force were preventing it from naming the place. Then it began to tap again quickly and softly.

"Semlin!"

Faltin pieced the message together. "A woman is dying

in the railroad-station at Semlin on the border between Hungary and Serbia."

There was one powerful blow: "Correct!"

Then the ouija began to dance around the table again. It really seemed as if our combined strength would not succeed in holding the light board still. It disclosed nothing else, but kept repeating over and over the one word, "Pray! Pray!"

We must pray for some poor soul on the border-line of death.

Then we dropped our hands and broke the current of communication for a while. Burda fell on his knees and piously recited the Lord's Prayer three times.

Schulhof began to question the tormented spirit again. "Are you present among us?"

"Yes."

"Can you tell us what disease you are suffering from?" The ouija spelt out, "P-a-i-n."

Schulhof asked again. Again "Pain" was the only reply.

Burda was deadly pale. "It's what we're doing that's paining her," he cried.

The ouija seemed to become enraged. It acted as though it would throw itself on the floor. Then it rapped out loudly the word, "Child."

We could not understand. Someone suggested that an elf or some other malicious sprite was in the table; for, according to spiritualist theory, the function of elves is to interrupt mortal communication with the dead. But in the meantime the significance of the two words had suddenly come to me.

"A woman is in labor-pains," I cried. "She is dying in childbirth."

The ouija responded with one satisfied knock: "Yes."

Schulhof bent tenderly over the board as though it were a sick-bed.

"Tell us if we can help you in any way," he said.

"Pray! Pray!"

"We will pray. But is there nothing else that can save you?"

"I don't know," came the answer.

"Can't any one of us here help you? I'll tell you their names. Ressl?"

"No."

"Sebastian?"

"No."

Then the ouija began to tap of its own accord, and named Adler. Until that moment my hand had not had the slightest thing to do with the answers to Schulhof's questions. Every answer had come to me as a surprise. It might all have been genuine, for all I know. For which one of us could have thought of such things? Like all the others, I experienced that shivery, tired feeling along the spinal cord, which is typical of séances. At the same time, all of us were on edge with an unhealthy sensation, a feverish excitement at being able to pry into God's mysteries without first having to pay death's unpleasant entrance-fee.

Again I heard Schulhof's solemn voice: "Answer us! How can Adler help you or save you?"

The ouija simply kept repeating the one word, "Pray!"

But, as it was beginning to spell out this word for the

second time, a light pressure of my hand changed the "pr"
into "w," and the "y" into a "d," while I added an "e."

"Wade!"

It was done like lightning and I did not stop to reflect on
my forgery or its meaning. The next letter, which I had
nothing to do with, was an "r." Without reflecting, I
quickly managed to spell out the word "river."

Then the ouija again spelt out two words without my
assistance.

"Sun . . . East . . ." Then it stood stock-still.

Burda read the message from his record: "Pray, Wade,
Sun, East."

We were not long in guessing its meaning. It was obvious. In order to save the unfortunate soul from present and
everlasting pain, Adler must wade into the river at sunrise
and pray, facing the east.

Bland was furious. "That's all damned nonsense," he
shouted, "and I think you're all crazy. Look out that you
get home safe to your own beds. Adler, you come with
me."

Ressl defended us very earnestly.

"Shut up, Bland," he said. "Neither you nor anybody
else knows what's been going on here. Or do you think
you do? Perhaps you'd like to give us a full explanation?
Maybe it's one thing and maybe it's something else. But
suppose a woman really is dying in the station at Semlin
and Adler can help her?"

Faltin was positive. "Certainly, she's in the station at
Semlin," he said.

I decided to take a hand in the discussion. "Look here,

Bland," I said, "be logical. Can you prove to me logically that there isn't a woman dying in the station at Semlin."

He turned on me. "I can prove to you logically that you're a lot of feeble-minded fools," he said.

"So you can't prove it, Bland," I said. "That's all I wanted to know."

Bland took Adler by the shoulders. "Don't do it," he said. "Remember your 'Frederick.' Have you forgotten that during vacation you promised me to remain an atheist?"

He seemed to be really troubled at the idea that Adler could break this solemn promise.

Schulhof put on a saintly expression. "Can you still be an atheist at heart after all this, Adler?" he asked. "It seems to me that we've just been given a real proof that God does exist."

Adler stared at Bland through his glasses. "No," he said at last, "I think that an atheist is a pretty foolish thing. . . ."

Meanwhile Ressl had produced two more bottles from the paternal wine-closet. Soon a wild orgy was in full swing. The thought of the woman in childbirth, dying there in Semlin, was the signal for this insane debauch. The more drunk we got, the more imperative it seemed to fulfill the dying woman's request. Bland still fought against it. It was all a trick, he said, or, if not that, some unconscious influence of our own minds. We howled the sceptic down with laughter. We solemnly asked Adler if he felt prepared to undertake the redemption of a human soul.

He had drunk a good deal himself, and he rose quietly.

It was nearly five o'clock in the morning when we broke up our party in the dawning light. As we were going out, Bland tried for the last time to dissuade Adler.

"Are you really going to do it?" he asked.

Adler gave me a quick look.

"Maybe," he said. "I'm not sure about it yet."

At that, Bland left without saying good-night.

We had to walk a good way; for, of course, the magic business had to take place at some point on the river outside the city. Befuddled with brandy and spirit-communications, we staggered along the empty streets, which seemed to be foreshortened by the vanishing darkness.

At last we reached the appointed spot, a few hundred feet upstream beyond the city-wharves. An old ferry-boat was falling to pieces at anchor in midstream. The little refreshment-booth on the bank was almost hidden from sight. The wind swept over the tangled river-grass. It was bitter-cold—the beginning of March. The first rays of the rising sun were beginning to gleam above the low range of hills on the farther shore. The rest of the sky was overspread with a greenish light.

Without a word from any of us, Adler silently stripped.

The river-water was dirty. The loathsome filth of the city floated on its surface.

The boy stood naked before us, so that for the first time we saw what his posture and his badly-cut clothes had previously concealed from us. His body was neither thin nor feeble, but firm and symmetrical. In our dazed condition we all marvelled at Adler's beauty.

He walked quietly to the river. He did not draw back. He entered the icy water as though he would not have changed it if he could. The blackness of the river-water was heightened by the lights of the beacons on its surface. Adler kept wading in deeper. The water was already up to his breast; and, if Burda had not suddenly cried out, he would have vanished into it completely. The thought ran through my mind: He's committing suicide. But when Burda screamed "Stop!" Adler stood still and raised his arms toward the east, to pray for that soul in Semlin, as had been commanded.

It was a strangely moving sight. Burda was blubbering prayers at my side. Faltin suddenly threw himself full-length on the ground. Even Ressl was sobbing. All of them were wrestling for the peace of that spirit in whose creation they had all probably had a hand. I stood watching them. A desolate sense of soberness was slowly breaking through my intoxication. It was day again.

· · · · ·

It is day again.

A few pages of scribbled paper are lying in front of me. I think that I am tired at last. My eyes are beginning to smart. What is written on these papers? No, I must not grow tired yet. I must not lie down. I could not sleep even if I did. What torture it would be to lie helpless in bed and have these disturbing visions flash before my eyes! I can't afford to grow tired for a long time yet. For to-morrow I must be prepared to face Adler. I must go over our whole past life. He may demand it of me! I'll make myself some black coffee.

CHAPTER V

DISTURBING visions!
A yellow bat is flitting across my window. At first I mistook it for a yellow butterfly. But it grew larger moment by moment. And now it is a golden heraldic bat that keeps flitting up and down before my eyes. I will pay no more attention to it. For all this is taking place in my mind, and is only the result of over-excitement!

I see enormous faces gliding by! Faces of moss, of rotting mold, heads with eyebrows of withered leaves, with noses of bark. . . . I don't have to close my eyes to see them. In fact, it is hard to keep from seeing them, they are so vivid.

Before me is lying a docket on which is written in big letters, "Murder of Klementine Feichtinger, Prostitute." Worms, caterpillars, and all kinds of loathsome creatures are crawling on that docket. But now I am beginning to see something entirely different. I see Adler.

I see a long stretch of path in a park. Adler is passing by me with that unmistakable walk of his. I follow him. But he gradually disappears, growing smaller and smaller, until he vanishes at the point where the parallel lines of the curbstones meet. Nothing else.

Adler is sitting in a remarkably unschool-like schoolroom. He is the teacher. It is obviously an American schoolroom. The boys sit informally around him on the floor. He is reading in a serious voice from a big book. But the boys are laughing. "Hello, Adler!" says one little fellow. Then I see nothing more.

A room! It must be Klementine Feichtinger's! She is standing before the mirror, in her chemise. In the mirror I see Adler, who seems to be throwing a big football at her. I am positive now he did it in a fit of revulsion.

The detention-ward of the prison! He is in Cell Twenty-Four. It is the cell for intellectuals. I know it very well. He is staring solemnly at the watery prison-broth, which he leaves untouched. Should I have food brought to him from a restaurant? He doesn't look as though he could afford it himself. Why do I sit here at my desk, instead of going to him at once? For that is my duty, and nothing else. . . .

Two cups of black coffee have given me new strength and have sharpened my perceptions. I feel as fresh as if I had slept eight hours. I must guard against any sort of capricious action. Let me not introduce any spurious causation into this affair! Let me above all be realistic, realistic and nothing else, with a keener and keener sense of realism. My task is not to confess my sins, to absolve or indict myself (I am not a public prosecutor). My task is to examine myself. Then we shall see. . . .

.　　.　　.　　.　　.

We simply could not talk about such things before Adler. Probably he would not have avoided them, for he avoided nothing. But when he was present, such talk simply died out. The atmosphere that seemed to envelop his nature, that delicate veil of solitude, made it impossible to go on talking about such things when he was present. He had long been a butt. Teachers and students both laughed at him, and yet there was not one of them who would have dared to talk smut before him.

I can't say that such conversation was especially attractive to me either. I know nothing more unpleasant than the sort of writing which, under pretense of revealing the subconscious, simply panders to the ruttish hankering of its author after smut. I always had to struggle against my natural instincts in order to feel at ease with the connoisseurs. It was difficult, but I conquered my feelings in this respect for I always strive to be agreeable. Besides, I had my own ideas about life, and I would have been ashamed not to have explored such a vast field of depravity.

Among the athletes in our class was a boy named Unzenberger. He was as stupid and as strong as an ox, and he was the class-hero; for the fact that he had to shave twice a week made him a sort of demigod of ripening manhood in our eyes. Unzenberger's powerful body, which was always threatening to break his seat in the schoolroom, exhaled a certain atmosphere of male coarseness which affected even some of the sensitive natures in the class. His throaty voice and mountain-dialect suggested bar-room brawls, beer-drinking, kisses bestowed on servant-girls, and hours spent in brothels. Ressl, the pampered boy, was not entirely immune to this masculine coarseness of Unzenberger's, although he had hardly ever exchanged a word with him. In Ressl, too, the superabundant sap was rising, though perhaps not quite as coarsely or rudely as in the peasant boy.

Schulhof was another case altogether. He belonged to those darlings of fortune whose nature never troubles them, and who therefore have the power to move women at all times and in all places. Men of his type are never shy, and always conscious of their power. They hardly ever change. Even as boys, they look like experienced men. They do not exactly grow old: they become played out. At sixteen they know all there is to know; at sixty they have learnt nothing more.

It was Ressl who first took me to that place which inspired me with so much more fear than pleasure, though I would never have confessed it for anything in the world. Now and again Schulhof went with us, indifferent and confident of success.

Women, for me, were divided into three classes. To the first class belonged those stately and elegant ladies in trim tailored dresses and a cloud of furs whom one frequently met on the streets. One saw them, too, in their low-necked evening-gowns, leaning on the rail of their boxes at the theatre. There was no way of reaching these unattainable creatures, not even in dreams. The idea of knowing them, of hearing their voices, was never for a moment within the range of possibility. Looking at them, one felt a softly dazzling, then a wonderful burning sensation and a kind of rapturous sadness—that was all. They belonged to other worlds, were so majestic, so remote, so much a heavenly order of beings, that it was hard to distinguish one of them from another. For me, at least, they were not individuals at all.

But Faltin, the boy with the wide lips and the thin arms, ventured to worship them after his own fashion. The daring boy specialized in his own type of adoration, so to speak. Ecstatically he would tell us how he had met the wife of the manufacturer X—— or the Baron Y—— in their automobiles. Without losing a second, he had boarded a street-car, in the heart-rending hope of meeting their auto-mobiles again in the park. In the park he had chosen an advantageous post, and, sure enough, he had the rapture of seeing the adored ones ride past him four whole times. Faltin's days were crowded with tremendous experiences and immense satisfactions. The removal of a cloak before a mirror, the glimpse of a fair shoulder, the twinkling of a tiny foot—were not these enough, and more than enough, when one had the joy of telling others about them?

The second class of women included girls of our own age or a very little older. These young ladies belonged to vari-ous families in the city who kept up a kind of social life. Even while we were still at school a few of us, usually Ressl, Adler, and I, used to be invited by the parents of these girls to various parties they were giving for their daughters. We were principally in demand for tennis-matches, though also occasionally for afternoon affairs and even balls. Of course, as the youngest guests, we played no very enviable rôle at such affairs, where mature men, college-students, and grown-up persons in general were in their glory.

Still, this was an approach, though a hopelessly formal one, to the world of women. We did, indeed, feel a little less shut out. The times were different then. The girls in their jackets used to stroll along the streets, giggling at one another, all of them clad in that peculiarly girlish kind of armor that is made up of timidity and purity and feminine calculation. They seemed to be demanding that we think them beautiful and adorable. But—we must never for a moment notice that that adorable beauty of theirs extended to their feet, their legs, their hips, their breasts—their whole body. At that time I strictly observed this platonic restriction.

The third and last class of women consisted of the inmates of those brothels to which Ressl had introduced me. The women were little more than naked forms of flesh, clutching us in a common embrace. They gave me no pleasure: they made me shudder with horror.

To me, at sixteen years of age, the possibilities of love in this strange world into which I had been born seemed limited to these three kinds of women.

Adler remained untroubled by such things. He seemed incorruptible. Lust played as small a part in his nature as vanity. He was different from us who were always demanding something from life, trying to capture it even while we knew that it was all dream-stuff and phantasy. Adler asked for nothing, needed nothing. But for this very reason life threatened to avenge itself on him all the more surely. Left in peace, he would simply bow his heavy head. He was rich indeed.

I was probably the only one who noticed the mild, scarcely perceptible affection that Adler had for Marianne. I have only come across this silent, worshipful attitude towards women once since—in a learned man whom many people consider a saint.

Marianne and Martha were two sisters of our acquaintance, creatures as pretty as a picture. Marianne, the elder, seemed to float along as she walked. She had glossy-black hair, which contrasted admirably with her dark-blue eyes. Falling in love with her was a fad which like all others was introduced among us by Ressl. But it was a fad that pierced my heart in particular and pierced it painfully deep.

Chance meetings with Marianne used to cause me palpitations and giddiness. If I happened to spy her from a distance on the street, my day was flooded with happiness. I used to pace up and down for long hours near her house, nourishing my hopes with the thought that I would presently see her come home. But even if she did not come, I had had my portion of bliss in waiting.

In the evening I would go with Ressl to the Gran Canon; and so bewildered were we at that time that we felt no contradiction between these things at all. Neither of them had anything to do with the other.

Twice every week we used to go to play on the broad courts at the Tennis Club. The girls were always surrounded by a swarm of adoring swains whom we took to be prodigious men of the world. How we admired and hated them! These officers and rich idlers, these gentlemen in their faultless white togs, never honored us schoolboys with so much as a glance. Even the girls wasted few words on us. And it was really far more comfortable that way; for all of us, even Schulhof, found conversation with them difficult. We could never find anything to talk about, and would sit and stammer out stupidities while we were tortured by the painful consciousness that we were perspiring heavily. In any case, it was pleasanter to look at the girls than to talk with them.

I was a good tennis-player, so that I often played doubles with the grown-ups. I felt exalted at such times. My ambition would rise and I would be almost beside myself with the sense of my own importance. There were many opportunities to play; for very often there was a dearth of partners, so that it was quite easy for all of us to make up sets of doubles.

Only Adler refused to take part. He would sit for hours

on the bench next the court where Marianne was playing, without saying a word to anyone. His near-sighted eyes would follow the play with a joyous attention that had not a trace of self-consciousness in it.

I believe that Adler was in truth a born artist and philosopher. He always found satisfaction merely in observing things without desiring to mingle in life. Whenever he watched me play, I could see how pleased he was with my skill. What was I to make of him? It was I, after all, who had begun that laughter which still made every gymnasium-class a hell for him. Yet he seemed neither tormented nor depressed at my skill in a game which he himself preferred not to play. For he knew that my skill in tennis was genuine, while he was never for a moment deceived by my other pretensions.

When none of the peerless cavaliers was present, it was the privilege of us schoolboys to escort the young ladies home from the Club.

The road used to seem endless to me in those days, as it ran from the hills down across the suspension-bridge, to pass into the foul air of the city-streets. The suspension-bridge smelled strongly of tar; and ever since then the ideas of "April" and "love" have been mysteriously connected in my mind with the smell of tar.

On one of those homeward journeys, full of a convulsive discomfort which I felt very keenly, and of an equally convulsive bliss of which I was not quite so keenly aware, I had walked a good part of the way beside Marianne. Ressl was strolling behind us, between Martha and another girl. In front of us, Adler was walking in his stiff way, his head bowed, self-sufficing.

I could feel Marianne's swift, ethereal gait in my very bones. At times, the tennis-racquet that she was swinging in her hand brushed my leg. She exhaled a faint odor, caused by the exertion of the game. I was struggling to find something to say. After all, it was my duty to make conversation with Marianne, accustomed as she was to the brilliant conversational flow of experienced and cultured men. But I could think of nothing to say. We had crossed the entire length of the bridge in dead silence before I managed to force out some stupidity, about our game, or the city, or the theatre. My words sounded unnatural on my lips. Their enthusiasm lacked sincerity and embarrassed me further. They felt like something round and hard on my tongue. They made no impression on her; they had no life in them. Instead, they seemed to drop like cannonballs that I could have rolled out of her way with my foot. After that effort my resources were exhausted for another long interval.

I looked at Adler's back. It was not for the sake of ridiculing him; it was my fatal predicament which prompted my meanness, as I pointed to him and imitated his walk. I had found my material for conversation.

"Look at him," I said. "Doesn't he make you want to burst out laughing?"

But Marianne simply tossed her head and made a face.

"I don't like people who make conversation at other people's expense."

Once something quite touching happened which Marianne did not understand. It was in the middle of a set of tennis, and the players were changing courts. At this inopportune moment, Adler rose from his place on the bench

and walked up to Marianne with his near-sighted gait. She
stopped impatiently. I saw Adler make her a jerky bow,
then stand silent for a while before he mumbled a few
words. Finally he handed the girl a small book, much
worn by handling. The book-mark sticking in it was a
long-stemmed, faded rose, whose petals, from some contrari-
ness or malice, began falling at that very moment. The
faded, spinsterish flower seemed the very symbol of Adler's
unlucky maladdress.

With a completely bewildered expression, Marianne took
the book from his hands. The gentlemen players smiled.
Adler, however, repeated his bow, and returned to his place
on the bench. I understood the whole incident. Adler was
making Marianne an offering of one of his favorite authors,
whom he had literally read to pieces. My first inclination
was to explain the meaning of his gift; but the cavaliers
were so sarcastically amused and so uncharitable, and the
general atmosphere was so constrained that I could not bring
myself to do it.

Later I happened to meet Marianne in the vestibule of the
Club. It was already rather late, and most of the players
had gone home. She was about to go to the locker-room to
dress for the street. But she stopped me.

"What does this mean?"

With a slightly embarrassed movement of her hands, she
showed me Adler's little book, which really was scarcely
any longer presentable. I cast a contemptuous glance at it.

" 'Colored Stones,' " I read. "Stifter is Adler's favorite
poet. He probably wants you to read the book, Fräulein
Marianne. . . ."

She turned over the pages listlessly.

"I don't know anything about Stifter."

"As a matter of fact, you haven't missed much. He's one of the dullest writers in the world. . . . He's full of nothing but frightfully good characters. . . . And then he's so dreadfully improving. . . . Do you like to be improved?"

"Improving! That's very bad," she decided.

"Besides, Stifter's mind really isn't like Adler's at all. I don't understand why Adler likes him."

Her hand was on the door-latch.

"One always has to be watching one's self when your friend's around."

"In what way do you mean, Marianne?"

"Why doesn't he ever say anything? I can imagine that some day he'll do something that nobody expects."

This from the young lady who I thought had never even noticed Adler's existence! It was already rather dark in the vestibule, and there was a strong smell of leather, a smell that always seems to me to have something brazen, almost obscene about it.

"I'd like your friend very well, quite well, in fact," Marianne observed, "if only he didn't have red hair!"

I made the stupid observation that this was hardly his fault. Schiller had also had red hair.

The smell of leather became more and more brazen. Marianne took her hand off the latch. She was ready to continue the conversation. I was torn by two contrary desires: one, "Oh, if this would only go on for ever!"; the other, "Oh, if I could only escape!" She stepped away from the door.

"You play a remarkably good game, Sebastian. Where did you learn to play so well?"

"In Vienna. I was always lucky in having good partners."

"Oh, of course—you come from Vienna!" And she repeated, with an ecstatic intonation in her voice, "Vienna."

I realized how much this word had raised my standing in her eyes. No longer was I a mere schoolboy to her.

"Oh," she sighed, "if I could only live in Vienna!"

"Why?"

"Oh, there are really no attractive young people here," she said; and smiling, added, "All the men here are a little like your friend Adler. . . ." She was standing close beside me now. "Look out that you don't become like all the rest. . . ."

I hardly dared to breathe. She was tapping with her finger on my hand.

"What do you say, shall we both become acrobats, and do a double act? I'm certainly no actress, but with your help we might make out very well."

I had no strength left for enthusiasm. Then the stupidity of the conversation seemed to strike her and she broke off abruptly.

"Don't forget our garden-party."

And she held my hand in hers a moment before she released it.

I staggered away in confusion from the first love-scene in my life.

The garden-party took place during the second week in May. Marianne's parents had rented one of the palace-gardens about the city in which to hold the affair for their daughters.

Nearly all of our crowd had been invited to attend.

There were at least two hundred in all at the party. I went with Ressl and Adler. All the usual amusements had been lavishly provided. Marquees had been erected under the ancient trees, with bowers and little champagne-booths. There were mock bottles with flowers. There was dancing in a sumptuous baroque pavilion, where a large orchestra thundered from the platform.

I asked Marianne for a waltz. In vain.

I recalled our love-scene and thought that I had a perfect right to dance with her.

I went to her a second and a third time. More refusals. Finally, the fifth time, she could no longer help herself, and had to grant my request. We waltzed around. But she would not say a word to me, and only remained in my arms as a matter of form. She kept her face turned away from me and toward one of her superior admirers, who continued his interrupted conversation with her by pursuing us around the hall throughout the entire waltz. Though my feelings were mortally wounded, I strove to find some grounds for excusing Marianne. Finally I succeeded in calming myself.

Later I met her in a secluded portion of the garden. She was sitting on a bench beside some spick-and-span dandy or other. She had on a bright lavender dress. (It looked very modern, for to my mind whatever she wore set the fashion.) But I did not like her now. She had crossed her legs and was beating time with one foot. This annoyed me. The elegant grown-up gentleman, who seemed to me to be no longer young (thirty years was a patriarchal age to me then), was telling her a story in which a number of aristocratic names were mingled. He spoke through his nose abstractedly, as though bored. I noticed this at once.

She, however, seemed to be fascinated by the gentleman's company. I meant to pass by them, but she called over to me.

"Sebastian, do you want to do me a real service?"

I did not stir.

"In the vestibule you'll find a letter for Herr von Radischovsky. Will you ask for the letter and bring it to us?"

She made the necessary social gesture:

"Oh, yes . . . this is Herr Sebastian. . . ."

The spruce person neither arose nor offered me his hand. He simply mumbled something about "a pleasure." Marianne felt obliged to justify my presence there.

"His father's some big personage or other. Court of Cassation or something of that sort. . . ."

My mouth felt dry. I did not know what to reply. But she, too, was speaking with a nasal twang now, and could not repress the desire to utter the banality, "One of my little ones."

I turned in the direction of the pavilion. But I never thought for a moment of doing her her "real service." No, indeed! Just let me find my hat and get away. Yet what would be the good of that? She would not even notice it! A savage desire was beating in my brain. "God, God, how can I, a dwarf, revenge myself on this goddess?"

Then I met Adler. As usual he was quite content "to loiter on the threshold of life." He did not dance. He said not a word to anyone.

I took his arm; I took refuge in his peace of mind. We wandered around for half an hour or so. Then we came to a lawn where a number of people were standing. Marianne had just come out of one of the tents. She was carrying a big plate of candy and asking the guests to have some of it.

I cannot exactly explain how I came to think of the stupid and unworthy means by which I planned to take revenge on Marianne.

"Have you any money?" I asked Adler suddenly.

He blinked in surprise.

"Don't you want any candy, Adler?"

"Yes, but why do I need any money?"

"If you haven't any, I'll help you out."

"I happen to have some today. But why . . ."

"You have to pay for whatever you take."

"But we're both guests!"

"We're guests, that's true. But look at that crowd of people. Do you know, I'm pretty sure that this is a benefit-party. The hostess herself is passing the plate. I can't see exactly what the other people are paying. But we don't want to look like fools. As I said, I'll be glad to help you out. But you ought to put at least ten kronen on the plate, though God only knows where the receipts go to."

I never doubted for a moment but that Adler, who was absolutely credulous in such matters, would obey. Marianne came to us also, and presented the plate of sweets. I waited. Adler, who because of his poor eyesight always bought things slowly and hesitatingly, took a tiny piece of chocolate and cautiously laid his only ten-kronen note on the plate. None of the things that I had expected to happen in the style of the Lady of the Camelias occurred. Marianne grew neither pale nor furious. She hesitated a moment, then she handed back Adler's money with a surprised smile that was almost one of amusement.

My senseless and stupid attempt to outrage her had failed. But to this day the memory of that embarrassing moment is so vivid to me that I grow ashamed whenever I think of it.

I looked at Adler. He had clenched his fists under his chin and was staring at the ground with a peculiar fixity. I found him in the same woebegone attitude several minutes later.

Towards evening I left the party, together with Schulhof. "I need money," he complained. "I'm absolutely flat."

I asked him to let me see a certain photograph he had managed to procure somewhere. It showed Marianne and Martha in masquerade-costumes. Marianne, dressed as a cavalier, was exposing her slender, girlish legs,—an unexplored mystery to us at that time. I bought the picture from Schulhof for six or seven kronen.

During recess at school next day I thought I noticed that Adler was trying to keep away from me. I asked him something, but he did not answer. I walked over to a group where he was standing. He turned away. A depressing sensation of loss and of emptiness overpowered me. I would have to struggle to win him back. During Professor Voivode's class, when everyone did as he pleased, I wrote Adler a letter. I don't remember now what was in the letter, except my fear of losing him, though of course I twisted everything about, reproaching him and accusing him. My letter was like a finger with which I was trying to prod him from behind.

After school Adler came to me. He said nothing about my letter, but we walked off together. For the first time in a long while I found myself walking home with him. With a fearful giddy feeling the thought came to me, "I've lost him."

I just managed to ask him in a faint voice, "Aren't you going to show me some of your recent work, Adler?"

He listened eagerly. He hesitated. This meant more to him than anything else I could have said. A year had gone by since he had read us any of his work. Not only had I destroyed his intellectual pre-eminence; I had detached all his friends from him as well. Even Bland was passing through a period (it was Stendhal and Oscar Wilde this time) in which he affected dandyism and tackled the problem of harmonizing his neckties and his socks with all the solid erudition of his nature. God was no longer a subject for discussion in his room. Elegant epigrams were the rage. The art of making epigrams consisted principally in perverting any well-known proverb. We befuddled ourselves with intellectual contortions of this sort: "He who gets caught, sets a trap for others." Even Bland had forsaken Adler.

I stood talking with Adler for a while in front of his house.

"It's a strange thing, Adler, but I've never been inside your house. I don't know how it looks at all. I haven't even the slightest idea how you live. I haven't any real idea of you. . . ."

"I know it," he said.

"And still we're friends, Adler. . . . I should really like you to read me your new things . . . alone up there in your own room."

I was afraid he was going to refuse me; for he considered a long while before he looked frankly at me and said, "Come this afternoon."

This, together with a thousand more things, is still alive in me. It would have died long ago had it remained what it was originally: the pervasive evil, the customary wolfish-ness that exists among human beings.

But these things live on because they led up to an actual crime, for which I should have been punished, even if there were no justice in this world and no statute of limitations. But is there any statute of limitations in the truest sense? And what about justice?

Adler read me two little prose works. One was called, "The World Comes into My Room Through the Window." It was a narrative whose meaning I did not entirely follow. It was written in a very odd style. In it there is a chimney-sweep who is walking on the ridge-pole of the opposite house, and at the same time he is in the poet's room, where he seems larger and grimier. Perhaps Adler intended to mean that reality is sometimes more real within ourselves than in itself.

I looked around the poet's room, into which I was now penetrating for the first time, though I had been his friend for a year and a half. Adler had kept not only me but all the others at a distance in a very strange way.

While not exactly small, the room had only one window. This overlooked a brick wall and a gloomy landscape of roofs, where the appearance of a chimney-sweep might assume really significant proportions. There was no table in front of the window. Instead there was a sewing-machine, which exhaled a smell of cloth and rancid oil. The room was very bare—a bed, a table, two chairs, and the picture of a man.

I should not have been able to live a day in it. But it suited Adler well enough. Several generations of "near-sighted" men had made this their home. Their inner life had been everything to them.

Adler had read softly and rapidly, as though afraid of being disturbed. Presently a woman's voice called from the adjoining room. He shrank together, then rose in his peculiarly stiff way and opened the door.

"It's I, mamma. How are you?"

"Who's with you?"

"Sebastian."

"I want to speak to him."

I had to go in to see her. Her room was large and somewhat barren, though cluttered with over-ornate things that seemed to be highly prized by their owner. A very large statue of a negro held the lamp. A withered palm was mouldering in one corner.

The widow Adler was in bed. She extended a moist, cold hand to me. She was obviously at odds with life. There was no trace of her son in her dark, lowering features. She hastened to take me into her confidence:

"I know who you are. You're the very person to appeal to his conscience."

"How do you mean, madam?"

She skipped from sentence to sentence, seldom finishing any of them:

"He's so impractical . . ."

"I beg pardon."

"No interest but in useless nonsense. . . . Push a chair up to the bed for him, Franz."

I sank deep into it. She went on preaching.

"Impractical people make their own beds and then have to lie in them. Just think what he could be doing! My brother is a gem of a man. He's always saying: 'Franz will go crazy before he's finished.' He doesn't sleep all night long."

Adler attempted to interrupt his mother. But there was no damming that torrent of complaint.

"I'm so worried about him, my dear Herr Sebastian. Sometimes I've had to lie here for weeks, just as you see me now. . . . If only I were well and had my health again! If only I could always be there to look out for the boy! . . . But I've always had to shoulder every burden alone. My sainted husband was just such another as this boy; and you know how he ended. The very living image of him! . . . He too was always pacing up and down, up and down; and if I'd ask him something suddenly, he'd jump, just like this boy. . . . A teacher! I tell you, being a teacher, with nothing but Latin to eat, means starvation to people as impractical as he is. . . . And he doesn't have to do it. . . . His uncle has a good business and is always saying to me, 'You'll see, Pauline, I'll make a man out of Franz yet.'"

Adler shook his head.

"I'll never go to uncle, mamma."

His words angered the woman.

"There, you see. Who knows whether you'll ever be a teacher or not? . . . Professor Kio says that you've fallen behind terribly, and that there's a bad end in store for you."

"Did you go to Kio, mamma?"

"Yes, I got nearly crazy with worry yesterday and went to the office. Professor Kio warned me you two had better keep away from each other. . . . You don't do each other any good, he says. . . . Franz will soon know why."

"I really don't know what Kio means, madam," I said. "Franz is either running out to walk the streets at night, or else he keeps pacing up and down in there. . . . When does he ever get any sleep? He'll get sick. . . . He'll go the same way his father went. . . . Oh, my God, if you could only have seen Franzie when he was a little boy! The sweetest child in all the world. . . . Everybody used to say so. . . . He had eyes as blue as heaven. . . . But he was impractical even then. . . . We used to take him to the baths every summer. . . . I tell you, things were different in those days. . . . One day we went for a walk in the fields. I was talking to my sainted husband when suddenly I saw that Franz was gone. The child had simply vanished. . . . Well, we hunted for hours. . . . I thought I'd go crazy, Herr Sebastian. The tears still come to my eyes when I think of it. . . . And where do you suppose we found him? Imagine, he was only four years old and he wasn't crying at all. No, not he; he was just gazing up at the sky and thinking. . . . He hadn't even noticed how many hours had gone by. . . . Impractical! You can't send a man like that out to face life alone. . . . I'm always dreaming about his being run over, crossing a street. . . . Oh, my God, my God!"

Adler was standing with his face averted. His mother went on crying wearily.

"I'm always thinking, of course, he's still young—but there's an end to that, too. I went into his room yesterday. He didn't even see me. . . . He was simply standing there crying and crying, just as true as I'm telling you, he was crying and crying all by himself. . . . My heart just stood still. I ran to him. . . . But he simply pushed me away. . . ."

"You don't have to tell that, mamma," Adler exclaimed. He ran out of the room.

"There, you see how it is," she moaned. "You see how it is." Then she let me escape too.

Adler tried to excuse his mother.

"She has a rather unfortunate disposition. Women have no sense of shame."

He said nothing more about the matter and we went away. He intended to read me his second work in one of the parks.

It was called, "Man as Pleasure-Lover and as a Source of Pleasure." It was a whole philosophy, or rather a theology, that Adler had developed from several points of view. Sooner or later all his ideas seemed to run to theology. In this, too, perhaps, he was simply the last of many generations of "near-sighted" men. I still remember stray ends of ideas and images from this essay, just as I do from Adler's "Frederick." I remember something about creation being "an abandoning of babies." God never took care of His world but exposed it without any provision. But the infant-world had to eat and drink, and, since God had neglected to provide for it, it had to suffer the curse of providing for itself, of devouring itself in eternal transmutations of matter, simply in order to exist. An inherent "cannibalism" permeates all life from top to bottom. But nature shuddered at its own inherent cannibalism, and, although one animal will devour another, there is a tendency among the more highly-developed orders to respect life in one's own species. Lions do not eat lions.

How Adler applied this train of thought to human beings I no longer remember. But the sentence, "The human being is distinguished from the rest of creation not by his reason, but by his appetites," still rings in my ear. "Man is the only creature that eats not only to appease its hunger, but also to tickle its palate." The human race discovered "seasoning" and at the same time discovered "sin." Cannibals eat human flesh, not because they have to, but by way of gourmandizing. Man is merely the most tasty of tidbits.

Then followed a profound and childlike plaint against man's higher, his spiritual cannibalism, against the lust to hurt and humiliate others, against the enjoyment of others' misfortunes. . . .

Was this philosophy of man as pleasure-lover directed against me personally? Were these few pages intended as a punishment for my "kneel down" in the confectioner's and for a hundred other base tricks? Was this the way that Adler's patient but triumphant spirit took to avenge itself?

But at that time I did not think of anything like this. I was not even conscious that I was Adler's enemy, his Iago. I thought of myself as his friend. I saw in him the boon-companion of my nights and days.

What discomfited me was Adler's genius, the scope of his mind, his logical force, the freshness of the pictures he drew, his images, but, above all, that intangible, that non-human genius, that he seemed to radiate. His nature was possessed of a singular sweetness which I resented. As always, when his superior qualities came to the fore, I was tortured with doubt and a longing to pull him down and exalt myself.

I walked home depressed and unhappy.

Ressl, Schulhof, and I had already gone five or six times to the Gran Canon. We had given a number of our friends a spirited and somewhat boastful description of our daring exploits, but that old sense of shame still prevented us from discussing them before Adler, or asking him to come with us on our adventures. Gradually I began to resent the advantage he had over me in his ignorance of those very exploits, the memory of which used to depress me every moment of the day, even while I was boasting of them.

One day I was walking with Schulhof and Ressl through the park on the hillside near the Tennis Club. We had not been asked to escort the young ladies home, as the grownups were performing this honorable service that day. Around one of the bends in the Serpentine Road, I had a glimpse of Marianne walking between two officers. I could distinguish the light swish of the gravel under her feet from the heavy tread of the men.

Ressl asked me something, but instead of answering him, I said, "It's a long time since we've been to the Gran Canon."

Our tastes had changed very quickly. Of course, the reading-circle was still in existence, and new members were being admitted from time to time, but our interest in it was pretty well played out. Our taste for night-life was gradually taking its place.

Ressl responded to my suggestion at once:

"We can go tomorrow. It's our turn to play hookey tomorrow anyway."

I had worked out a complete system, according to which no more than three boys would ever be absent from classes at one time, so that we would not be suspected.

"Who is the third man off tomorrow?" Schulhof asked.

I consulted my memorandum-book. It began very imposingly with a list of teachers and students. Then it passed on to more shady matters. Written in secret symbols was the record of my visits to the Gran Canon. My relations with Marianne, their increasing warmth and sudden cooling, were represented by a strongly varying barometric curve. I turned over these pages hastily, to find the table by which I regulated the hookey-system for the entire school.

It was Adler's turn to be the third man absent; but Schulhof explained that he would like to go with us that night to the Gran Canon. He was used to late hours, he said, and the lack of sleep would not bother him. I hesitated. "Perhaps we ought to take Adler with us once," I said.

Schulhof objected. "What do you want with Adler?" he said. "He'll die as pure as Joan of Arc."

Suddenly Ressl's rosy cheeks turned pale with fear.

"My God! Kio!"

True enough, Professor Kio was coming up the Serpentine Road. As usual, he was wearing his gray overcoat, with the frayed hip-pockets. He wore a brown "melon," dark gloves and a cane. I noticed that on his left arm there was a mourning-band, which he never wore at school. And how different his walk, from that to which we were accustomed in the classroom! Then he strode through the room like a whirlwind! Now he was plodding slowly and wearily up the hill. He was out for a promenade, to use his own phrase. We snatched our hats from our heads. Ressl dropped his cigarette behind his back. When Kio recognized us, he cast a slow glance at us. It seemed to be made up of suspicion, a mild contempt, and sorrow, strangely blended. Then he returned our salute with the most elaborate bow imaginable. Human worth, that had been his governing idea all his life! Even students in the seventh form, whom one could not trust out of one's sight for a moment, were worthy of a certain measure of respect.

My first thought was, "He's seen us! We'll have to think up a very clever lie for tomorrow, if we're going to make our absence sound reasonable."

After a pause Schulhof turned to gaze after Kio. "He hasn't been the old Kio for two years," he said.

"What do you mean?"

"Well, it was before your time, Sebastian. You'd have to have seen it to appreciate it. What do you say, Ressl? Remember how he used to enact the capture of Maglaj? The desk was a wall, the pointer was a sword, and Komarek had to be the insurgents. We used to have good times in those days! We used to hide in terror under our seats. . . ."

"Well, what happened?"

"Don't you know? Kio's only son died two years ago. He was a lieutenant of hussars. Kio was away from school for two weeks. When he did come back, I tell you, nobody would ever have recognized him. Before that he used to make us sit up and take notice, I can tell you—Lord, the zeros came thick and fast. But now he's only a shadow of his former self."

Ressl seemed to be thinking of something else all this while.

"Adler!" he said, suddenly. "That *would* be a lark!"

The Gran Canon was a night-club and very skilful at concealing its real business. It consisted of a café and bar, and also several upper stories whose mysteries were known to the initiated. The café was fitted out with a red carpet and hung with Japanese lanterns. There was rather dubious champagne to be had, bad liqueurs, and good beer, cocktails, and black coffee. Women, dressed not as waitresses, but in evening-gowns, served the guests and sat down at their tables. One could dance with these women to the false notes of Goldner, the piano player. On longer acquaintance, a number of the girls, who had rooms in the upper storey, would show an inclination to receive gentlemen callers.

Ewald Ressl, the Munich mystagogue, had introduced his sixteen-year-old brother to the night-life not only of the spirit-world, but to that of the city as well. Shortly afterwards Ressl introduced me in turn to this paradise.

Ressl prided himself on his boldness and on his clever way with the women, and acted as though he had been a familiar guest at the Gran Canon for years. He carried himself with a rather loud assurance, even when many other guests were present, and with a lordly air would summon to his table Marfa or any of the girls in whose favor he was basking at the moment.

Schulhof comported himself with almost the same assurance. But his behavior was very different from Ressl's. He simply acted as if he were perfectly at home there, as if he

considered the guests as nothing, and valued only the enter-
tainers in that weird, nocturnal society.

Of course, the theatre, which he had rather forsaken of
late, was recruited in a large measure from the same calling,
so Schulhof did not come altogether as a stranger to the
Gran Canon. He loved to discuss their private lives with
the girls. He would gossip for hours with the villainous
head-waiter. The pianist was his bosom friend. If in a
good humor, he would make witty remarks, drop silver
coins down the girls' blouses, and then hunt for them before he gave them away. In fact, he acted like a member
of the establishment.

My own behavior was considerably more restrained than
my companions'. If I could simply sit quietly in the restaurant, feeling no need of aping the dash and boldness of the
others, I was content.

Adler entered the room with us without any suspicion.
Ressl immediately began to put on airs. They knew who
he was, the son of a Croesus. The pianist bowed low. Because of his lovely voice, they used to call Schulhof Caruso,
whose star at that time was just beginning to rise. Goldner
played a well-known aria, while "Caruso" stood beside him
in an arrogant pose, and sang.

I turned to look at Adler.

He glanced around indifferently at first, and without
grasping the situation, but gradually a slight discomfort became more and more apparent in his manner. He avoided
looking at the stout, half-naked women who were strolling
about the room.

I felt the same repugnance for these creatures, as well as
for the mingled stench of nicotine, cheap perfumes, and

acrid perspiration. I thought of the photograph of Marianne and Martha in my coat-pocket. There was still time to leave the café and take Adler with me. . . .

At that moment, Ressl, who had rifled his father's wallet that morning, ordered wine. Marfa seated herself between Adler and Ressl.

"Did you pawn your schoolbooks that you're so big-hearted?" she screeched. She had guessed right. Except for Homer and the Tacitus I used in Kio's class, I had hardly any schoolbooks left.

Marfa was by far the best-looking of the women at the Gran Canon. At least she had a trim figure and sound teeth. But her voice was ruined. It was as ravaged by tobacco-fumes as the air at the Gran Canon at five o'clock in the morning. She could no longer speak softly.

"You must have some marvellous parents," she screeched. "Oh, wouldn't I give it to you, Ressl! You ought to be laid across somebody's knee and given twenty-five smacks, that's about what you're looking for, sweetheart!"

"Wouldn't you rather take *him* on your knee, Marfa?" Ressl suggested.

Marfa surveyed Adler from head to foot.

"So you've brought me a new one. What a cherub he is!" Delighted by this name, she screamed it again, "A cherub!" Adler tried to force a good-natured smile, but he had to hide his face in confusion. Marfa clutched his arm.

"You're certainly no beauty, cherub, but there's room in your head, there's something inside it, at least. He's an intelligent cherub. The rest of you are common swine."

Marfa, who was no longer exactly a welcome guest at our table, burst into a sudden fit of rage.

"You're common swine," she screamed, "nothing but common swine! I'm only taking on intelligent men. Do you hear me, Ressl? You gold-lined, lousy scoundrel, you're no cherub. And you, Caruso, you're a glib-tongued high-flier with your pomade, but you're no cherub either. And that quiet fellow there, with his pretty little hands, I'll keep my eye on him, the sneak, the pot of dish-water. You look like the kind that would kiss while you're sticking someone in the back, you overgrown hypocrite of a parson, with your long, pointed nose. . . ."

The head-waiter strolled over to our table and bent over the intoxicated girl. "Don't insult our guests, Marfa," he said. "How often do I have to tell you that?"

But she simply beat on the table.

"I don't like it when people don't tell me their names! Everybody here's going to tell me his name—right away! The cherub's going to tell me his name, too. No, never mind, I don't want anything from him, because he's a cherub. . . ."

Ressl jumped up and began to dance around. "Seduce your cherub, Marfa! He's yours."

But Marfa kept screeching, "I don't want elegant gentlemen, I only want intelligent ones."

Cognac was served. We mixed it with the champagne. Marfa kept her hold on Adler, who was making himself as small as possible. I still remember how his eyebrows twitched. He gulped his drink hurriedly, probably so as not to spoil the sport. But so much female flesh near him seemed to make him unusually shy.

Ressl brandished a bank-note:

"Seduce him, Marfa. I'll stand treat."

He dropped the bank-note down the woman's neck as if he had been a rich peasant's son with silver buttons on his coat.

I was still smarting from Marfa's attack. I wanted to prove that I was not a little sneak, not a pot of dirty dish-water, not a coward, not a hypocritical parson, but a real man. With this end in view, I bet Schulhof that I could drain a tumbler full of cognac at one draught. I won the bet. As a result I gradually began to lose my senses. I only remember that I kept staring fixedly at Adler and solemnly declaring over and over again, "The world comes into your room through the window."

The world seemed to be a gigantic chimney-sweep who stepped from roof to roof and crawled into Adler's room.

Presently I found myself in a dark stairway. Schulhof had disappeared. Ressl was close beside me. My first words were, "Where is Adler?"

Ressl pressed my arm. "Upstairs," he said. "She dragged him along."

My head was in a whirl. "Quick, let's go up," I said. "I must see him, have a look at him." I managed to force out a long, bold laugh, as though some particularly good joke were ahead of us. But I did not feel much like laughing. Ressl tried to hold me back.

"You're dead-drunk, Sebastian."

But I was not as drunk as he imagined. I knew very clearly that I wanted to see Adler at all costs.

"The whole thing is queer," I heard Ressl saying in a dejected and guilty voice. "Usually he never drinks a drop, and today he's drunk more than all the rest of us. I'm afraid he's drunk too much."

I pulled Ressl along with me. He knew where Marfa's room was. I would not let go of his hand in the darkness. Finally we found ourselves in an empty parlor full of horrible plush furniture. I hunted for a way out, found a door, and pushed it open. There was a portière in front of it, which I pushed aside.

Adler was sitting on the bed in his underclothes. A big, naked woman was kneeling in front of him. Her head was nestling in his lap. He was repeating over and over, softly, "No, no, please go away, please go away."

Ressl, who could not see anything, pushed me a little, so that both of us fell into the room. With an indescribable scream, Adler leapt up from the bed. He glared at us like a wild beast. His screams did not cease. His forehead was blood-red. Marfa flew to us. She tried to hide behind my back. Adler had seized a three-panel boudoir-mirror and was glaring at us with the unconscious eyes of a murderer, with eyes in which there was no longer any trace of himself. Only primal terror was there, defending itself against brutality! Then his screams grew less shrill. Gradually he sank to the floor and began to sob and weep, as uncontrollably as he had before been screaming.

The mirror folded up suddenly with a bang. We were not drunk now. Fear clutched at our hearts. We saw that the weeping boy was not in his right mind. Hysterical words were mingled with his sobs. Our hands were ice-cold with fear. We lifted him up. We spoke to him.

"Be quiet, Adler. It's all only a stupid joke. Just laugh at it. Come now, pull yourself together."

But the drunken hysteria did not leave him. Marfa

brought water. Ressl's face was twisted with terror. What would happen if the attack did not pass off, if we had to have a doctor . . . ? He kept imploring, "Pull yourself together, Adler, stop this fooling."

Too much naked flesh, I thought, and asked Marfa to go out of the room. She had hardly gone before his sobbing became quieter. We brought him his clothes. He began to put them on, shivering. We helped him like frightened thieves. Then we led him downstairs and hurriedly left the house.

It was early morning. The sun shone wanly. We were standing, befuddled, in the city-square. The market-booths were open, and the men were unloading big baskets full of vegetables, flowers, and fruit from the country-wagons. The women fruit-sellers were scolding, and their angry little eyes stared at us idlers with hatred. Buyers were going to and fro among the stands, handling the ripe fruit and scrutinizing it with sleepy eyes.

Adler stood still, breathing-in the morning-air. Ressl had his arm around his shoulders. "Can you see all right now?" he asked. "Now everything's all right again. The whole business was a joke. There was really nothing to it at all."

Adler inhaled the air. It was still pure and unsullied. At last he smiled slowly in forgiveness. I nodded quickly to Ressl:

"Let's take a cab and ride along the park-drive for an hour or so. Then we can go to the baths and afterwards we'll have a wonderful breakfast."

Adler was gradually becoming himself again. He heard

my remark. He basked like a convalescent in the sunshine.
"Yes, let's do that," he said. "That's a very good idea. . . ."

Ressl led him forward cautiously. There would be plenty
of cabs near the station.

I would follow them right away, I said.

I was a little dizzy, and felt a strong desire to be alone
for a few minutes, after the experiences of that night. The
merry-go-round began to turn dismally in the market-place.
I leaned against the wall of a house.

Suddenly I realized that Komarek was standing before
me. I saw that he had been watching us for a long while.
He had a market-basket in his hand, over the top of which
a head of cabbage was peeping.

"Aha!" I thought. "So Komarek has to buy the provi-
sions for the family before he goes to school in the morning. . . ."

But his lowering head, with its bitter, proletarian eyes,
kept staring quietly and insolently into my face.

"What are you waiting here for?" he asked.

I was so exhausted that I turned on him sharply.

"What business is it of yours?"

He did not stir at all. He was silent. But those proletarian eyes kept staring fixedly at me, and grew deeper and
darker with contempt. Then he lifted his hand, very slowly,
very quietly, very deliberately, and slapped me in the face.
Was I too tired to spring at him? Too tired to avenge the
insult, or too cowardly? My cheek burned from his blow.
I leaned against the house and marvelled at myself. Am I
deceiving myself now, when I say that his blow felt pleasant
to me?

Komarek waited for a moment, enjoying the effect of his

blow. Then he turned about thoughtfully and walked away. He had punished me without knowing why himself. Perhaps only because at that moment he happened to compare his life with mine.

It was the first and only blow I ever took in my life.

Komarek need not hide it from God.

CHAPTER VI

KIO paced grimly back and forth in the middle aisle between the rows of seats. Suddenly he stopped and
tiptoed softly up behind Adler.

"Continue reading at the place where we left off."

Adler moved his heavy head a little, sighed, and dropped
off to sleep again.

A burst of laughter came from every row.

"Silence!" roared Kio so earnestly that a dead silence instantly spread through the room. He seized the sleeping
boy by the shoulders and wrenched him from his seat. Then
he marched up to his desk, his heavy military footfalls echoing on the floor.

"Come here, Adler."

The boy advanced into the vastness between the teacher's
desk and those of the pupils. There he, and we, heard the
following doom pronounced:

"The day after tomorrow the last faculty-meeting of the
year will be held. The dice have been thrown and you have
lost the game, Adler. I have gathered this much from all
my colleagues. You, for whom I once prophesied so splendid a career, have succeeded in competing with Komarek
for the lowest grade in the class. There are still others on
whom justice will descend," he went on. "Yes, Ressl, you
have good cause to hide behind the man in front of you.
And, Sebastian, your innocent face doesn't deceive me for

140

a single moment. It's the curse of evil deeds, an innocent face like yours. I have thirty years of teaching-experience behind me, and those innocent faces are an open secret to me now. It would be far better for you to put on a guilty face and throw yourself into your work at the last moment. For the ship is sinking. Let whoever can, save himself! *Si fractus illabatur orbis, impavidum ferient ruinae.* But enough of that. Horace belongs to a higher class than most of you will ever reach."

Suddenly his personal sorrow was poured forth in words:

"In the earlier part of the year I congratulated myself on having a class of clever boys whom I would be able to send proudly, one and all, into the practical life that lies ahead of them in the form of a university-career or a year of volunteer-service in the army. You have turned my joy to bitterness. If I could, I would be rid of you today. I am an old man; and every hour I am giving you all that I possess. And you, who are young, respond to my effort with inattention, with talking, with joking, with whisperings behind the desks, and scribbling on top of the desks, and a hundred other tricks. *Sunt pueri; pueri, pueri puerilia tractant.* But you are no longer boys. Quite the contrary, I'm afraid."

Then his glance fell again on Adler, who was standing motionless before the desk. Kio spoke from the bottom of his heart:

"And you dare to fall asleep under my very eyes. You dare to insult me with this impudent inattention, I, who received the highest honor for courage on the bitter soil of Bosnia at the taking of Maglaj! There are a number of things going on in this class that cannot well bear the light of day. Every day two or three of you are sick or absent because of something the matter at home. How does this strike me? It strikes me as it would a hospital-clerk reading over a list of patients. But this is an imperial academy and not a sick-ward! . . . As for you, Adler, you can take this much for granted. There's no more hope for you. Get out your pilgrim's staff as quickly as possible. The faculty washes its hands of you. Even the German instructor, Professor Stowasser, says your writings are immature, pretentious, and conceited. They have turned him against you. The history-instructor, Voivode, has been unsuccessful in interceding for you. I myself can do nothing more for you. And I will do nothing more for a man who thanks me by falling asleep during my class. Familiarize yourself with your fate at once, you have nobody but yourself to thank for it. Already I've put out my hand too often to save you. *Sapienti sat*. Today is Friday. The faculty will meet on Monday to decide the life and death of a number of others besides. Be so good as to ask your guardian to see me Tuesday. Now be seated!"

The deathly silence continued. Everyone felt that this philippic was something more than an angry harangue on Kio's part—that his heart really was breaking. He remained silent and did not return to Tacitus. His grim and gloomy glance, like that of an old general who is watching his own defeat in battle, wandered through the transparent window-panes and rested on the dismal façade of the lodging house opposite.

We had carried things too far. Our constant absences from school, our nocturnal excursions into spiritualism, our drinking, our bar-room visits, had, as was my intention, brought anarchy into the class and a hundred little details had betrayed it to the teachers. Added to this was a certain intellectual bumptiousness. Ought the followers of the modern Parnassians, whose daring names flowed so glibly from our lips, be compelled to describe the sequence of the action in Schiller's *Wilhelm Tell?* To questions of this sort there was only one answer possible for us—contemptuous silence. During the class in exact science, which we were told, "has nothing to do with practical life," attentiveness on our part would have seemed hypocritical to us. Not only Adler, but the whole class dropped behind. Even the first-violin, "Fischer, Robert," sounded off-key, so surrounded was he by our influence; for the best conductor in the world is lost in a bad orchestra. It was our ambition to lead an exciting private life at the same time that we were at school. If my neighbor Burda, a born son of duty, tried to study his lesson, I used to pinch him until he gave up his undignified zeal. We used to sit in class reading periodicals, writing letters, twisting proverbs into impudent paradoxes, drawing caricatures, sending one another epigrams, and waiting in tortured suspense for the bell which would release us.

Even now it is something of a mystery how we boys succeeded in spending so many nights away from home. Circumstances strangely favored our zeal to taste life. Ressl's parents lived in a huge palace in the city, where supervision of their son's whereabouts would have been impossible without a warden. Adler's mother was seriously ill, a bed-ridden woman. Schulhof, whose parents lived in a small town, stayed at a *pension.* I myself had a charming room on the second floor, right above my aunts' apartments. I could come and go unnoticed whenever I pleased. Soon after my arrival I wheedled the key out of the old house-keeper, who loved to pamper me.

Now the catastrophe was clamoring at our door.

The faculty had decided to offer up at least one victim to Orcus, in order to stem the growing lack of discipline in the class. Adler seemed made for such a sacrifice—this boy whose huge head was veiled in the shadow that had fallen on him—this boy without guile or malice of any kind, so easy to crush, to annihilate.

Kio and Voivode would have fought for him, but these old-timers were weak and futile against the new men who had come to us at the beginning of the term.

Stowasser, the German instructor, the strongly nationalist fraternity-man, hated Adler. He hated his "intellectual" style, which, he declared, was insolent and confused. Without any further comment, he ran his pencil from one side of Adler's compositions to the other, and added a note: "Completely unsatisfactory." But Professor Stowasser would not have succeeded in his attempt, which was obviously unjust, if the embitterment of the other teachers and Adler's almost morbid defenselessness had not helped him.

Kio's low-pitched, surly voice brought the Latin-class to an end. But Adler sat motionless, his head bent, solemnly staring at Tacitus's *Germania*. After the noon-bell, we were in the habit of gathering in a delicatessen-store near St. Nikolaus Academy. Today Adler and I sat alone at the table. Kio's thunderbolts had spread panic and had frightened the others away. That natural human cowardice in the face of catastrophe, that effort to make one's self too small to be seen, that firm intention not to know anything that may incriminate one, all were betrayed in the sudden defection of our comrades. They had hurried dutifully home, to creep into their various corners and learn better for the future. The charmed circle, which men draw about every victim, had already been drawn around Adler. He sat staring at the table, his face as white as wax.

"It's all over with me on Tuesday," he said. "My mother has already passed judgment on me. My uncle will put me in his store before vacation. . . . I'll be buried for ever."

I tried to comfort him:

"It's only the last week in May now, Adler. School doesn't end until the fifteenth of July. That gives you seven whole weeks. By that time a lot of things may change."

But he simply answered, "I have to go to Kio with my guardian on Tuesday."

"Wait," I counselled. "Simply tell him that your uncle is travelling. Your mother is sick. If any letters or bad reports come, we can get hold of them first."

"Why try to hold off the inevitable? It will come out sooner or later anyway. I'll kill myself or sell dry-goods."

He seized the liqueur-glass in his fist.

"No! I tell you, I'll never, never work for that creature."

"Kill yourself?" The words sounded grave on my lips. "You know you always have plenty of time to kill yourself, right up to the last minute. What we have to think about now is what to do."

Previously everything that had happened in Adler's life had been a spiritual experience; the security of his outer life had never been disturbed. He was a schoolboy like the rest of us, and free to go his own way. But now his security had suddenly been shattered at a single blow. Life was casting him amongst its odds and ends, where his uncle, and the others like him, felt at home and wanted to make a man out of him!

The only vicious emotion that I had ever observed in Adler was his hatred for his guardian, and this was exaggerated by fear. Adler described him as a greedy scoundrel, pathetically vain about his business, convinced that his shop and his daily proverb were world-shaking affairs which only the inherent unrighteousness of the times prevented from bringing him greater honor. That anyone should not want to enter the ranks of the dry-goods dealers seemed weak-mindedness to him, or something worse; at least in his nephew's case—a boy who wanted to go to college for no other reason than to make more beggars out of beggars' sons.

According to Adler, the uncle hated him; for whenever they met at home or on the street, he always had some slighting remark on the tip of his tongue. "Where did you get that high forehead, Franz?" he would ask. "Bourgeois romantic, eh?" Or, "Do young people always have to wear glasses? You can thank your father for that. He could never see two inches in front of his nose." But the saddest part of all was that Adler's mother, who really did love him, would use his uncle's arguments against him all day long. She had allied herself with the arch-enemy to annihilate her son for his own good in the world.

School had given Adler a chance to live a little longer. It was a breathing-space for him, a blessed interval; and through it lay all hope of future salvation.

Now this was finished and done with.

Although I knew it would go hard with me, too, and

though my own fate was more than doubtful, I was full of pity for Adler's tragedy at that moment. Ah! There are no tragedies in adult life that approach in frightfulness the tragedies of youth! For the weapons of smiling indifference are not given to youth. Such sayings as "It will pass over" and "There's nothing in the world as important as that" are known to the grown man, but not to the boy. How often does a child go to pieces in mortal terror! And there is no protection for him under the law.

Adler repeated, "I don't see how I can go on living."

Then I had an idea that sent a cold shiver down my back. "Listen, Adler," I said, "I have an idea, an idea for a crime. . . ."

After I had uttered these words, it was some time before I could continue: "Fischer must have taken the class-register from the classroom into the faculty-room. Do you follow me, Adler?"

He kept staring fixedly at the oilcloth on the table.

"The class-register isn't locked up in the desk now, as it was yesterday, but is lying open in the faculty-room."

At this point he lifted his head.

"What the faculty says isn't so important, Adler. The important thing is the register. For the conference can only take action on the basis of your marks. Do you see what I'm driving at now? We'll have to use the greatest care in changing a failure to a passing-mark here and there. But that's all that it's necessary to do. And you know, Adler, I have an ink-eradicator that will erase anything."

He was panting, and had gripped my hand so tightly that his nails cut me.

"Maybe I'll commit this crime for your sake, Adler, but

it's certainly no joking-matter. It's a crime all right! It doesn't come under the head of misdemeanors, but under the criminal code. Falsifying a document! When you're grown up you can get three or four years for such an offense. You know that yourself. But we'll see, maybe I'll do it for you. . . ."

My courage was still pretty weak.

"I've often made fun of you, Adler, but it's your mistake, not mine, if you haven't given me tit for tat. You may have thought sometimes that I wasn't your friend. But you see how your admirers, Bland and Burda, have de-camped. Now perhaps you can see who your real friend is. Come, let's go."

The street was gay with bright summer-color. Crowds of schoolboys from all the different grades rushed by, late for class. The clock in the tower at St. Nikolaus struck half-past twelve. In a conspiratorial whisper I commanded Adler to meet me at seven o'clock in the dark interior of the church. The idea of a church seemed to harmonize with the style of my plan. Then I sent him away. No one must see us together. Perils were already sprouting out of the earth on all sides. Adler obeyed me in silence, like a sub-ordinate. In silence we parted from each other.

I felt an intoxicating thrill of adventure, while I was sustained by the righteous feeling that I was about to commit a crime for another's sake.

When I entered the church at half-past six, Adler was already there. As a precaution, I carried a note-book full of Latin home-work in my hand. I kept feeling in my pocket for the little bottle of eradicator which could magically change every mark. I quickly instructed Adler to follow me to the school a few minutes later, and, if he met anyone, to pretend he had left a book in the classroom. Then he was to slip into the faculty-room, where I would be waiting for him.

The school-door was locked—the first unexpected obstacle. I rang. The janitor looked distrustfully at me. I felt my body gradually growing moist. Yet I had no difficulty in pretending impatience and haste.

"Listen, Pettner, I have to go up to the faculty-room to hand in this note-book."

"The faculty-room is closed after school is out. I can't let anyone in. . . ."

"Why, Pettner, what do you mean by telling me a thing like that. Kio ordered me to hand in this note-book. He's coming back later to correct it."

"All right; then wait down here for him."

"Why should I wait down here? What do you mean by locking me out? Do you think I want to waste my whole evening here? Let me in. Kio will expect to find it when he gets here."

I was trembling for fear the janitor would ask me for the note-book in order to give it to Kio when he arrived; but he only said, "Students in the faculty-room—that's a new one on me."

"My God, Pettner, if you're going to act this way, I'll simply go away, and you can get out of the row as best you can! You know Kio, though!"

I had pressed forward to the foot of the stairs.

"By the way, Pettner, it seems to me that I still owe you for the last time I had a drink at your house. . . ."

A voice from the basement called, "Father!" and, thank

God, Pettner gave up the struggle. "The faculty-room is still open," he said. "We haven't cleaned it yet."

Then Adler came along and mumbled his little speech inaudibly. Grumbling resignedly, the old man let us in.

The fatal room lay at the end of a passage that had formerly been an alcove. The door was standing wide open, and the pails and brooms of the charwomen had not yet been cleared away. The deed would have to be done post-haste.

On the big green table all eight class-registers, greenish-grey folios lay piled, one on top of the other. With a sweep of my hand I had ours at the window, where there was still a spot of light on the little drawing-table. Outside I could see scurrying masses of clouds with reddish-yellow edges, like the edges of wounds. I saw ghastly objects lying around—school-furnishings which had been brought there to be repaired, a snake, and a stuffed ape.

I naturally opened to my own name first. The disclosures were melancholy enough, but there was no actual failing-mark. If we had time, I might even be able to raise my own average. I got out my crime-implements, the bottle of eradicator, the dabber, and the sponge. Then I turned to Adler's name.

He was leaning against me, peering over my shoulder, but I drove him away.

"For God's sake, watch the door," I said.

First I went over his mathematics-marks. "Three failures," I called out to him. "One we'll let stand, and we'll change the other two to passing."

"Thank you," Adler whispered back idiotically. I myself had grown quite calm. I was pervaded by a feeling of indolent courage, as though I had unlimited time and leisure for my work. Here, in the very citadel of the no-smoking edict, I hurriedly lit a cigarette. I placed a few drops of the eradicator on the failures and waited until the ink had disappeared. By this time Adler was leaning over my shoulder again. Again I drove him away. Then I took the blotter. The first failure vanished without leaving a trace.

But at that moment I felt an overweening and insolent desire to tempt fate and torture Adler with my cold-bloodedness. The gruesome possibility that the janitor might come back was keeping his nerves on edge. Suddenly I interrupted my work and began to whistle and to hunt for an ash-tray—in that room, of all places! When I turned around, Kio was standing before me. I had never given a thought to the private circular staircase which only the faculty used.

I had no feeling of being stunned by a sudden blow. What I felt was a slight sensation of panic that seemed to leave a peculiar bitter-sweet taste in my mouth.

My first thought was, "What will Adler do?" Anyone else who had had the luck not to be seen would have breathed a prayer of thanks to heaven and cut and run. But Adler walked right into the room.

Kio did not say a word. He did not even look at us. He paced back and forth with tremendous strides, his unconscious hands picking up all sorts of objects, which he stared at with a savage fixity. We saw the veins in his temples swell till they stood out like jagged streaks of lightning. With a crash he hurled into the closet the book that he had been holding in his hand—Gindely's "Modern History for Secondary Schools." Then he began to stride back and forth again. Finally he came to a halt in front of me, and, his voice trembling with loathing, said, "You smell of tobacco," while, with a furious gesture, as though he wanted to hurl me into the street, he flung open the window. Meanwhile the drop of fluid on the second failure had swelled to a big blue blot.

Still Kio said nothing. He had sat down, and was staring out at the church-spire.

"Sebastian," he said hoarsely.

"What is it, Professor?"

He simply pointed limply and wearily toward the door.

We went out of the room.

"You go on," I commanded Adler, once we were outside the door. "Two can't do any good here now. I'll get hold of him myself."

I stopped at the next street-corner; but I had to wait there fully an hour. When Kio did come, he acted as though he did not see me, and paid no attention to my salute. I did not dare to approach him. I had lost all my courage.

But I followed him, in such a way that he could not notice me while I did not lose sight of him. The streets seemed a confusion of night-crowds. The world had taken on a totally new appearance. The drab, indifferent human throngs swept past me, and were so far removed from what I felt that I seemed to stride apart, veiled in a misty shroud of destiny, a destiny that was forcing me to act and, at the same time, was numbing me like a strong drink of punch. Who would save me? Yet I would not for anything have foregone this feeling of terrible suspense, this voluptuous stupefaction.

Every criminologist has observed the remarkable cheerfulness frequently evinced by criminals shortly after their arrest. I felt something of that sort when I was still very young, first experiencing it during that walk.

Sometimes I would lose sight of Kio. But I would quickly find him again. Presently he turned into quieter streets. He crossed through traffic to buy a newspaper. I disappeared into a doorway, so that he would not spy me as he entered his house. But he stopped in front of a narrow doorway and waited. Had he known that I was following him all the time? I glided nearer. Without turning towards me, he addressed the dark vestibule: "Follow me!"

Creaking stairs in a dingy dwelling! Kio led me into a dark room. A hollow sound, as he lit the light, a sound out of my vanished childhood!

So, after all, Jupiter lived in a room!

He seemed to have a wife, too, for a long-drawn "Emil!" issued from the kitchen.

The four walls were hung with etchings depicting exciting moments in the Bosnian campaign, while under them hung an enlarged photograph of a young man. Over it was a palm-branch. An old officer's sword was standing in one corner. On the desk were several high piles of Latin and Greek composition-books. Many were lying open, showing the bloody traces of grammatical battles. That night, the first in which I may be said really to have lived, I felt keenly the commonplace pathos of all those note-books.

Jupiter put on a house-jacket.

"Sit down."

I sat down on the edge of a chair.

"Do you know your father's position?"

"Yes, Sir."

"He is the chief justice of the supreme court."

"Chief justice of the supreme court," he mused. "In other words, his Excellency is judge over all other judges, and hence judge over all other men in Austria. Am I not right?"

"Yes, Sir."

"Your father decides in the case of every legal judgment against a citizen that is brought before him. Answer me, am I right?"

"Yes, Sir."

"And if a judgment against an evil-doer is brought before your father, even though the evil-doer is his own son, what must he do?"

"Professor . . ."

"I am asking you, what must his Excellency do?"

"Sir . . ."

"He must pass judgment, though it cause him agony."

"I've . . ."

"You've nothing to say whatever, Sebastian; for I, like your father, can do nothing now but let the law take its course."

"But I'm not guilty of anything, Professor Kio."

Kio took my bottle of eradicator in his hand and read aloud the label: "Destroys ink. Obliterates every trace of writing in a few seconds."

"But that bottle isn't mine."

"To whom does it belong, then?"

"I don't know."

"What were you looking for in the faculty-room?"

"We—that is, Adler and I—were on our way to the class-room to get a book that we'd forgotten. But we saw the faculty-room door open and went in out of curiosity."

"You don't say! And was it curiosity that tempted you to open the class-register?"

I kept silent.

"And was it more curiosity that made you commit the common crime of forgery?"

"I didn't do it."

Kio's voice rang out again magisterially. "It would be better for you if you didn't try to lie to me."

I could hardly draw breath to say, "I'm not guilty."

"You mean to imply that Adler committed this crime?"

Again I kept silent. I felt dull and hollow inside. My sole idea was to clear myself in the easiest and simplest way. Kio was neither my teacher nor my judge now. Suddenly he turned on me sharply.

"I expect you to deny that implication," he said, as though it were a point of honor between us.

I kept silent.

"Sebastian," he exclaimed, *"Homo sum, nil humani a me alienum puto.* Do you understand me?"

"Yes, Sir."

"But where dishonor and deceit begin, at that point the *homo* in me ceases to exist."

I was hardly conscious of my own words as I said, "But it wasn't my name."

Kio sprang up and dashed out of the room. But he returned again the next moment. During the entire conversation I had been staring at the picture of the young man in the lieutenant's uniform. Without knowing why, I took refuge in this photograph, as though it could bring me help. Kio noticed this and grew more and more nervous. But as soon as I felt that my gaze was troubling him, I stared all the harder at the lieutenant. Kio was silently striding to and fro again in the room. Suddenly he stopped short, with a stamp of his foot, and, with the same furious gesture with which he had flung open the school-window, wrenched the picture from its hook and set it face to the wall. He had to pace up and down a long while before he grew calm. Then he asked softly, speaking over his shoulder, "Are you willing to give me a written statement that Adler is guilty?"

I did not answer. After a while I saw Kio's well-known writing on a white sheet of paper. I signed it, as though I were writing in a dream. Kio thrust the paper to one side without looking at it again. This, and a number of other details, should have shown me plainly enough that Kio did not intend to prosecute, but save us. But I was no longer capable of such observations.

Kio seemed alarmed by my appearance. He came up to me and laid his cold hand on my forehead.

"Would you like a glass of milk?"

He himself brought me the milk from the kitchen. I drank it, with his strangely tragic face bending close to mine.

A night of deep sleep followed. Next morning everybody felt that some great event had transpired, though none of us discussed it.

Every community instinctively grows feverish when one of its members is sick or threatened by some danger. In the same way the seventh form at St. Nikolaus grew excited without knowing exactly what had happened. But for most of the boys it was a pleasant excitement, for the poignant anticipation of catastrophe was in the air, and there are always more spectators than victims in this world. Ressl and Schulhof hung inquisitively around me. They asked discreet questions. I buried myself in Homer.

Faltin, however, acted most strangely of all. He was the finest seismograph imaginable for such an upheaval. But he was almost too sensitive a magnetic needle and indicated all kinds of wild happenings. Instead of recording one, he recorded several. A hundred speculations and rumors radiated from his seat through the entire class. We had been caught in the Gran Canon. . . . We had been discovered playing hookey. . . . Komarek had threatened to beat Professor Stowasser with a club. Each of these rumors, for a time at least, was accepted as gospel-truth. For Faltin's very soul was aquiver with creative excitement. After the noon-recess he rushed into the room shouting, "They are all in with the old man—with the principal!"

Of course, this happened very often. But now it took on a portentous significance. Faltin immediately vanished again, to resume his eavesdropping. A minute later, his head was thrust through the door once more.

"Stowasser has just gone away," he announced.

It was a harmless fact, but one that immediately resulted in a general uneasiness. Faltin slammed the door behind him with a bang. But he tore it open at least ten times more, to shout some splendid premonition of coming disaster into the room. Adler and I sat quietly, not speaking to each other or to anybody else.

In the middle of another class, Kio strode into the room. Suddenly everyone sat up very straight. He spoke abruptly.

"I want Adler and Sebastian to come to me in the office at noon on Monday."

From that moment on, Adler and I were as though hand-cuffed together, like secret conspirators. Even those boys who had so often bragged of their contempt for school—even Schulhof and Ressl—prudently kept their distance. We were left absolutely alone.

We remained alone in my own room. My aunts had gone to spend Saturday and Sunday with friends in the country, as they often did in the spring. I did not have the courage to confess my cowardly lie to Adler. I simply told him that Kio knew all. It would only have embarrassed both of us without making things different. But I con-stantly caught myself thinking that if only Adler would vanish from the face of the earth everything would turn out all right for me. I had given a proof of my innocence ready-made into Kio's hands. They could not prove my guilt from my side of the class-register.

But Adler was still on the scene! And no power on earth could make him disappear. I drew pitiless pictures of the future. In his office on Monday, Kio would command us to appear before the faculty. A few hours later, the hearing would take place under the supervision of the principal. No amount of denial would help then, for the *corpus delicti*, the blue blot in the class-register, was perfectly visible. Even if they wanted to, Kio and Voivode could not defend us or hush up the affair. Judgment would be passed; that is to say, a statement of our misdemeanor would be forwarded to the higher educational authorities, who would hand down the final decision of expulsion. In the interim, before the inevitable judgment was handed down, we would be prohibited from attending any further classes, so that the other boys might be shielded from the influence of criminal elements. Then, before a week had passed, "Fischer, Robert," blushing with shame, would call at our homes, to command us to appear at the Academy at such and such a time. At the sentencing of an ordinary victim, only the principal was usually present; but for this mournful occasion, which would be solemnized like a national holiday in the big gymnasium, the whole school, the entire faculty and student body, even the pupils in the lowest grades, perhaps even their parents or guardians, would have to attend. Formal dress would be prescribed, of course. Aunt Aurelia would come in her widow's weeds. Adler's mother, perhaps, would be wheeled into the hall in her invalid's chair. Then the principal would call upon us. He would stand on a specially-constructed platform decorated with palms. In our hands he would place the shameful documents that would bar us for all time from St. Nikolaus Academy and all other secondary schools. At that moment, I added, the singing-teacher would probably strike a few chords on the organ, the parents or guardians would take out their pocket-handkerchiefs, while the school-choir would sing, "Eternal Honor Heaven Adores."

But the tragedy would by no means be ended with that act. In fact, it would last as long as we lived. We would be barred for ever from attending a university. I could never be a lawyer, never be a government official, as my father wanted me to be, and which was the only career open for me. The chief justice of the supreme court would realize that his son was a dangerous criminal, so that I really could not blame him if he should order me to take some other name than his. He himself would probably start proceedings to change my name, and probably superintend them personally. Of course, I need never expect to receive another cent from him. Even my aunts would be forbidden to support me. Adler, on the other hand, I said, might thank his stars that his uncle was willing to take him into his dry-goods store as a clerk without wages. The uncle probably would do no worse than make remarks like "You've got to be an educated man to keep my books straight, my boy!" And when he was twenty or forty or sixty years old, he'd still be clerking without wages. . . .

It was eleven o'clock on Sunday morning when I proposed that we take another sip from the cup of life and solemnize one last soul-feast before the axe fell. We set out to visit the scene of my first love for Marianne—for the last time in this life, as I thought.

Just as we arrived, a sudden pelting shower came on and raised a cloud of powdery dust on the neighboring fields. We saw that everyone had taken refuge in the club-restaurant. The club-house was empty. Again I smelt that shameless odor of leather, that acrid smell of tanned putrefaction. I pushed open the door to the women's dressing-room. Adler was terrified. But, unable to hold me back, he followed me. There was not a soul in the room, only a tantalizing silence and neatness. There was not a hat or a piece of clothing on any of the racks. All the lockers were closed and there was absolutely nothing to remind me of women.

But in the middle of the inner room were two little shoes.

They seemed extremely lifelike, standing there, one close beside the other—the overpowering vision of a woman's foot, far more arousing than reality. I could control myself no longer, and uttered a cry. It was no outbreak of sentimental tears; it was the cry of a galley-slave, embittered by life, that burst from my lips. Then I suppose I began to moan, for Adler came to me and clasped my hands in affectionate helplessness. But he saw merely that I was crying, and not that I was enraged. He saw tears, the sorrow of a soul, but not Sebastian, not me, not my secret feelings. I pushed him away, and, hurling myself at the shoes, tore off a buckle.

Marianne had just come in with two other women, but luckily had seen nothing.

"What are you doing here?" she asked severely.

Overnight I had changed completely. There was not a trace of shyness left in me.

"We're looking for you, Marianne."

She was obviously surprised at the tone of my voice, but followed us out of the club-house. The rain had stopped. I looked boldly at her, something I had never done before. She wore her white sports-costume, with a raincoat over it.

"We've come to say farewell to you, Marianne."

"I do not understand. Are you going on a trip?"

"Trip or not, there'll be plenty of excitement about a number of things soon. Give a friendly thought to us sometimes."

I felt clearly that I was making a bad impression—that she disliked me. She immediately became a patronizing lady talking to two boys.

"I hope I'll never have to think of you in any other way."

"Oh, don't underestimate the importance of such thoughts. It takes more courage than one might think to confess that one has known certain people. I don't know whether you possess such courage or not, Marianne."

"I still don't grasp what you're driving at."

I went on with growing exaltation. "People like that happen along every so often. Today they're mere nothings, loathsome outcasts, good-for-nothings whom nobody wastes a glance on. The next day they astonish the world. Then we like to remember them. Something's going to happen soon. . . ."

She looked bored. "I think you'd do better if you spent more time on your schoolbooks," she said.

"Do you still take us for schoolboys, Marianne?"

"Yes, I most certainly do."

"Well, then, I can tell you in secret that since yesterday we're schoolboys no more. We have been doomed for life. Isn't that true, Adler?"

"Yes, that's true," he said.

She looked at him. He stood there forlorn and desolate, like a blind young boy. His face was quite pale.

A feeling of motherly pity welled up in Marianne.

"Is your friend sick?"

"No sicker than I am. We both have the same disease."

"No," she said, "I don't believe that. There's nothing the least bit pitiable about you. But something's really wrong with him. Why don't they take better care of him?"

A real torrent of insolence burst from me at her words. "Marianne," I began, "I must gratefully decline your offer to do acrobatics with you. I haven't the time."

At first she did not say anything. Then she replied rather uneasily, "I never intended to become an acrobat."

The buckle of her shoe was burning into my hand. I felt a kind of mad courage. If she had stood there a moment longer, I should have thrown my arms around her and taken her to me. But she went softly up the steps. "I must go in," she said.

She gave me her hand quickly. But when Adler made his bow, she ran her hand over his hair with a gentle, indescribably caressing motion.

In an ugly silence I crossed the bridge with Adler on our homeward walk. We stopped, as we had often done before, at a favorite spot, and peered down at the grey water, combed into foam, like dirty white hair. I resumed the recital of our miseries.

"Our expulsion is by no means the end of it all, Adler," I went on. "Maybe our case will go before a higher body than the national board of education. Maybe it will go to the juvenile courts. And then they'll stick us in some reform-school, in some hell. . . . What do you think about it?"

Adler reflected for a long time, and then he said, "It's not only possible, it's very likely."

At home they informed us that "Fischer, Robert" had been there to deliver a message from Professor Kio to me. He had waited for an hour or so, and then had gone to the other gentleman's, to Adler's. But he would not return that night.

We sat down, our bodies numb with fear, facing each other.

"That's the beginning of the end, Adler."

A fleeting hope gleamed in his eyes. "Suppose it's good news!" he suggested.

"How can it be good?" I asked. "A summons to appear in school the first thing in the morning is the best thing we can hope for."

"But suppose he only wants to talk to us?"

"Our examination will take place soon enough, never fear."

"Do you think I should go home, Sebastian?"

"Go home? Why, your mother has had the letter for hours! Your uncle must be with her already. Of course, if you really want to, the pleasure is all yours."

Despair broke from him, as he said, "No, I can never go home now." And he buried his head in his arms.

It was six o'clock when we gradually began to entertain the idea of suicide. It was I who first suggested it. Adler was lying on the divan in my room. The idea seemed to make him happy. He had been waiting for it like a salvation he did not dare think of. So natural did death seem to him that he did not show the slightest sign of surprise. Even I was not at all afraid. I felt fiercely tense, as though something extremely interesting lay just ahead of me, some journey, some thrilling adventure.

Everything had suddenly taken on a new and more significant meaning. Student suicides! We were no longer mere criminals. All the blame would fall on the teachers. The newspapers would take up our cause. The faculty would be dismissed after severe censure. The school would be closed. Speeches would be made at our graves. We would become heroes, gory victims of tyranny, exalted beyond all the Ressls, the Faltins, the Burdas of this world. . . .

But Adler had little understanding of such feelings. He began to speculate about the way in which we should do the deed. It was better not to be alive in the morning. But we did not possess a weapon of any kind. Besides, a revolver might imply that one of us was a murderer. We could not procure poison of any sort. Adler had an aversion to hanging himself. Illuminating-gas was the only alternative.

We decided to remove the shade and the mantle from the desk-lamp in my room. We bolted the door and locked the window. Then we had to consider whether or not to leave letters behind us. At first I wanted to leave some solemn "Last Letter to Mankind." But Adler declared that the idea was disgusting. Later I urged that each of us should leave a letter with the following wording: "I withdraw voluntarily from life."

Then I proposed that Adler should lie fully clothed on my bed. I chose the divan for myself.

Adler was already lying down. He was in haste. Then I opened the gas-jet. I went quickly to the wash-basin to tidy myself for death. I put a fresh part in my hair, having first rubbed it with grease, so that my death-struggles would not rumple it. Everything was ready. I lay silently on the divan, like a knight on his tomb. It had grown dark.

Was Adler already sleeping? I shouted into the dark, "Adler, can you recite a passage from your 'Frederick?'"

There was no answer. He was asleep.

Then a voice came from the other side of the room. I

could not see his big head or his vacant eyes, so that it might as well have been a disembodied voice reciting:

"Pronounce, O priest, pronounce anathema,
Pronounce it, crush that which has long been crushed;
The Ocean dances guiltless by the cliffs."

"Go on."

"Nonsense, it's foolishness," he said.

" 'The Ocean dances guiltless by the cliffs. . . .' That's perfect, Adler. You see I'd never have imagined it like that. I would simply have written, 'The Ocean laps the cliffs. . . .' Ah me, I'd never have written that! But you put the whole picture in that one line. The ocean is a girl or a woman. She wears something white, a light sports-costume. No, not so; it's a mull dress she's wearing. And she's dancing quietly all alone, all by herself below the cliffs. A disgusting old cliff—I can see our school-principal plainly—and she's dancing a satyr-dance around the cliffs. She can make a curtsey, too. The sea keeps receding with little curtseys. Adler, decline *mar, maris,* stem *mar.* That's the same stem as in Mary. Do you suppose the sea is connected with the Virgin Mary in some way? Or at least with the name Mary. . . ."

"Star of the sea," Adler said. "It's quite likely. . . . But let's get to sleep."

"Listen, I think I've made a philological discovery. Fischer would never have thought of the connection between the sea and all the Marys in the world. He's nothing but an echo, a dud. He reeks with definitions: 'Words of curiosity, information, memory, division, power, and fullness take the genitive.' It would never have occurred to him that 'genitive' has the same stem as 'genitals,' would it? But that's why his report-card is like a virgin dressed in pure white. . . ."

"Sleep," said Adler.

" 'Guiltless.' . . . That's the loveliest of your poems, Adler."

"Do you think so?"

"Do you feel any effects yet?"

"None."

"I don't either."

"It will be some time before we do."

"Do you know that you're much more gifted than I am, Adler? Your 'Frederick' is a work of genius. . . ."

"Nonsense," he said, "it's quite immature. Now, let's keep quiet."

"I'll tell you something, dear Adler. You get up and go away. Let me be the one to die here. How can this whole affair harm you in any way? Put all the blame on me to-morrow. Tell them that you didn't know anything about the whole business. And then forget it all. You're a genius, and some day you'll get the Nobel Prize. As for me, I'm nothing. . . ."

I heard Adler make a movement in the dark as though he had turned toward me. But I could not see anything. Then suddenly I seemed to be gazing into the pupils of his honest eyes.

"You're nothing, are you, Sebastian?" he said. "Yours is a different case from mine entirely. We ought to have a long talk about it. . . . But what's the use of long talks now . . . ? It's all the same to us now. . . . Let's keep quiet and go to sleep."

There was no further answer.

The gas purred on with a gentle sound. It was as if the element of time had become audible—with a monotonous, purring hum.

Suddenly I sat up with a jerk. What folly this was anyhow! I called softly to my companion in death. He was sleeping quietly and did not stir.

If I should go out of the room now, if I should leave him there, he would vanish from the face of the earth, and I would be saved. Then there would be no one left to prove that I forged the marks. No one could prove that I knew anything about his suicide, either. I would simply go out of the house and not return till midnight, when everything would be over. Who would ever say that I had murdered him? (Only, I must be careful to destroy my farewell-letter.)

We had simply gone to my room to study our lessons together. About seven o'clock my head had begun to ache and I went out for a walk. Before I went out, I had asked Adler to spend the night with me, and told him to make himself at home in my room, since I intended to stay out some time, in order to get rid of my headache. . . . A flawless alibi!

I walked to where Adler was sleeping, in the soft radiance of the street-lamp, which was now lighted. He was sleeping with his mouth half-open. He had taken off his glasses. His face in the light looked beautiful. I slipped stealthily out of the room. Stealthily I closed the door behind me.

The house seemed vast and lonely to me. It was Sunday evening, and Agnes (the housekeeper), and all my aunts' maids had gone out. I did not have the courage to leave this house of death. The piano was open. While my friend was meeting his end upstairs, I sat down at the piano and struck some strange discords. My head was almost lying on the keys, and I said to the black and white ivories, "The Ocean dances guiltless round the cliffs."

But I would still need money. Where could I get money now? Above all, where could I get as much money as this kind of a situation called for?

Aurelia used to lock a good deal of jewelry away in her clothes-press. I remembered the basket, with all the different keys, that she kept in her bedroom. Probably one of them would open the press.

One of them did open it. I picked out a big antique earring.

While I was accomplishing this feat, my heart was thrilled not so much with fear as with another sensation. Until then I had never thought of my aunts as women at all, but simply as aunts. Yet while I was plundering Aurelia's bedroom, I became aware of the strangely reticent life of these two women—of the exquisite order of their clothes-press, at once so immaculate and so shameless, with its fabrics as unreal as lies and its little handkerchiefs that were almost non-existent. I noticed for the first time all the vials and toilet-articles that I had so often seen before. Oh, yes, Aurelia was already thirty-four. With my plunder in one hand, and with Adler upstairs dying, I leisurely pulled open mysterious drawers, only to discover a feminine confusion of curling-irons, nail-files, hair-pins, thimbles, gloves without mates, cotton bags, tattered letters, bills, patches of cloth to be quilted, and many other strange things.

How much time had really elapsed? An hour, or ten minutes? As I left my aunt's bedroom a wild terror swept over me. Everything grew dark. I did not dare light a lamp.

I must fly upstairs and into my room! A heavy wave of gas poured out at me. I flung open the window.

"Get up," I cried, shaking Adler. "You can't do it this way. Get up, you've got to get out of here."

But Adler did not wake up. Perhaps he was already dead. I tried to lift him up.

"You must get out of here," I kept repeating. "You've got to start on a journey."

But he simply fell back inert. At last, however, he sat up on the edge of the bed, with his eyes shut.

"You must get away, Adler."

He yawned slowly and then said languidly, "Of course you really *aren't* gifted, Sebastian. . . ."

"Come to the window," I said. "Get up."

"Your poems, dear Sebastian—after all, you've only translated them. . . . They sound so, so . . . French. . . ."

I succeeded in getting him to the window. I held his head out into the fresh air as though into cool water.

"It was so nice and beautiful," he kept muttering bewilderedly. "Everything was going so nicely, why did you have to do this? Why did you wake us up?"

"Be quiet, Adler," I said. "You mustn't die. I have a better idea."

His eyebrows were contracted by a spasm. "Let me alone, for God's sake! Your ideas have proved terrible enough to me already. . . ."

He began to revive. I led him down into the parlor. I helped him into an easy-chair. I lit the lamp and gave him a cigarette.

"Smoke, so you don't fall asleep again. We'll eat and drink something."

I found half a bottle of wine and some fruit-cake in the kitchen. But by the time I returned to the parlor, Adler had dropped his cigarette. There was a burnt spot on the carpet. Then he ate up the whole cake. He was getting better. "Can you hear me now, Adler?" I pleaded.

"Yes, yes, of course I can."

"I've really got a great idea that will save your life. As things stand now, no matter what happens, you'll have to go to your uncle. Wouldn't it be better if you simply escaped, ran away . . . ?"

He looked at me slowly.

"And what about you?"

"Oh, me? My father's a powerful man, and they'll never push my case to the limit. The fact that you've run away will help things. There'll be danger of a terrible scandal. They'll hush everything up."

Adler hunted hurriedly through his pockets. "I can't even run away," he said.

I dangled the earring before him. "It's worth a thousand kronen."

He half rose. "You stole that earring from your aunt," he cried.

"What has that to do with you?"

"But they'll suspect the housemaids."

"That's none of my business, and needn't be any of yours, either."

"I won't take it."

"That's stupid. You can make it up later. Besides, you'll get money for it."

He struggled to find other excuses. "I can't pack my things. I can't go home."

"I'll give you my own travelling-bag, Adler, and everything you need, besides."

I ran up to the attic, seized my travelling-bag, and rushed back to my room. Without stopping to reflect, I threw all my clothes, coats, shoes, even my new smoking-jacket, of which I was very proud, into the bag. I even remember searching long and desperately for an unused tooth-brush which I knew was somewhere in the room.

Adler had dropped off to sleep again when I returned. I pulled him out of the easy-chair. "Let's lie down again upstairs," he mumbled, "falling asleep is much nicer than anything else can be. . . ."

"He must get out on the street," I thought, "and get some fresh air in his lungs."

Then we began to wander aimlessly through the dark. I held on to the heavy travelling-bag with one hand and grasped Adler with the other. I had the feeling that I was lugging along a corpse, a murdered body in a sack. But a corpse, even a beloved corpse, must be got rid of. I did not dare to stop talking. All night long I would have to talk incessantly, without ever stopping. The important thing was to keep awake all night. I must constantly keep thinking: "He must go!"

I led Adler into a passageway and began to present the case to him. "This isn't the first time that we've discussed a plan of escape for you, Adler," I began. "I've simply taken up the idea that you suggested yourself. Do you remember? You *do* remember, don't you?"

While I was speaking, I kept hearing Adler's mother saying: "You can't send Franz out into the world alone. In my dreams I'm always seeing him run over, crossing the street." Of course, he could just as well be run over here in this city. What was the difference, after all? It was no reason why I should sacrifice myself. He must go away. He must!

I babbled on. "Didn't you tell me about some sympathetic relatives you have in Hamburg who might help you against your uncle? Of course, they'd only be a stopping-place for you. I don't think I'd stay with those people. It might cause very disagreeable developments for both of us. But, in case of need, I wouldn't want you to feel that you're all alone in the world. You see, I'm saying Hamburg simply for sentimental reasons, instead of Paris or London, which, of course, are much more interesting cities. If I were in your place, I'd stay a few days in Hamburg. But after that, Adler, don't fail to take the first boat for America."

"For America," he repeated, leaning against the lowered shutter of a store-window.

I thought from the tone of his voice that he was getting more accustomed to the idea of going away.

I waxed enthusiastic, for his benefit. "America!" I exclaimed. "There's no more Wild West romanticism about it now. Men of your type have a chance to become great there now. Men of talent are highly appreciated there, because there are so few of them. I read it somewhere. And democracy, Adler, think of democracy! You have a great future ahead of you, while I have to remain behind here, a wretched European. Besides, America or not, it makes no real difference. I don't pretend to give you advice. Why, in a week you'll know much more about the world than I do. You ought to be happy, Adler. Comfort me, tell me that you're happy, Adler."

He shook his head. "Happy?" he said. "What have I got to be happy about?"

"You don't have to worry about money. Of course, money is absolutely essential; but for the present, at least, you'll have plenty. You'll have enough to travel like a gentleman and live in ease for a couple of months. What follows you can take care of yourself. With a little discretion you'll soon make good connections. But you must remember to write to me. And I can help you out now and then myself. Only, please don't write me at home, but through the general delivery. Who knows but they'll search our rooms. Simply put 'Comrade in arms' on the envelope."

I was paying hardly any attention to what I said myself. The problem of getting the money was terrifying me. It was ten o'clock of a Sunday night. Who would buy the stolen earring from me or tell me where to find a purchaser? Ressl, Schulhof, Faltin? Impossible! They were mere boys, incapable of serious deeds. Since yesterday I had outgrown them. I would have to find a man somewhere.

Like a chord, sounding deeper and deeper, Komarek's name kept ringing in my ears. Yes, Komarek, who had slapped my face for me, was a man, the only one who could help me. But where did he live? I recalled the vegetable-market where he had suddenly appeared with his shopping-basket. Then, as in a trance, I remembered his street and house-number, which, like the addresses of all the other students, was read aloud by the teacher at the beginning of every year.

Again I picked up the hand-bag and began to lead Adler on.

Komarek's house lay in a crowded quarter of the old city that has long been demolished. I stowed Adler and the travelling-bag in a little saloon. It was hard to find the right door among so many. But at last a voice did call shrilly through the darkness, "August, here's somebody says he wants to speak to you."

Presently Komarek stood before me in his shirt-sleeves, collarless. Faces were peering at us from all sides. Invisible slippered feet kept padding up and down the stairs. I had thought that it would be easier for me.

My voice sounded unfamiliar and obsequious, as I said, "Please come out on the stairs a minute."

He followed me over to the dismal light.

"What do you want?"

"Komarek," I said, "Adler has got to get away."

"Well, who's keeping him?"

"Komarek, there's no one else but you I can go to in this horrible business."

"What do you want me to do, kiss you for that?"

"I don't want you to kiss me, but I want you to stop and think what you did to me."

He looked up at the light and said nothing. A few of the peering faces had ventured half-way down the staircase by that time. I could make out the inquisitive, thin-cheeked faces of half-grown girls, Komarek's sisters probably. I had to speak distinctly and softly.

"Something dreadful has happened. You all felt it yesterday at school. Adler has done something dreadful. . . ."

"Oh, yes," he said, "one of you always has to do something dreadful before you think anything's wrong. I never do anything dreadful, and yet they flunk me."

"What do you want? You'll come through all right, and after the examinations you'll get your diploma. But ours is a different question entirely. It's a question of life and death, Komarek. Expulsion is the least part of it; but a trial, the law, jail. . . ."

My eyes were full of tears. Komarek simply stared at the light, as he said: "What has that got to do with me? Thank God, I've got nothing to do with it."

"But you can, you must help me," I said. "Adler must leave by the five-thirty express in the morning, for Germany."

"Why don't you go?" His distrustful smile was fixed on me.

"You'll find out tomorrow, between eight and twelve, when I have to face the whole dreadful business myself. But Adler's going to save himself. Promise not to betray us."

Then Komarek spoke seriously. It was a matter of principle with him.

"You're no friends of mine, but the faculty are my enemies."

"We need money," I said, "a lot of money. This earring has to be sold right away. Help us sell it, Komarek!"

"But suppose I tell on you," he said, in a leisurely, indifferent tone.

"You won't. I'm not afraid. You wouldn't do that."

He took the jewel and held it up to the light. The peering, gliding shadows stirred with curiosity. Komarek's hands looked very expert and very ancient.

"Jolowitz . . ." he said.

Then he disappeared, and returned fully dressed to lead me through the maze of alleys.

Jolowitz was sitting bowed over an illustrated periodical. He was reading "La Beauté de la Femme." How fearless Komarek was, and what a lot he must have been through to be able to withstand the silence of this cranky old man, who did not even notice our presence! Komarek laid the earring on the table without a word.

"I need money," I began; but Komarek thrust me angrily to one side.

Then Jolowitz began to scurry around his enchanted castle. He pressed the navel of a nude figure, and the eyes were illuminated within. He started an orchestrion playing, so that the room was peppered with the Radetzky March. I took refuge in my great weariness, as in a sentry-box. I heard words shouted loudly, as in a depot, when the train is about to start. "Old-fashioned setting. . . . It wouldn't be worth the bother. . . . Your parents, my young friend. . . . Sign this. . . ." The Radetzky March sounded above the haggling like the patter of rain.

At last I was holding a great many hundred kronen in my hand, an immense amount of money, according to my notions.

"Do promise not to say anything, Komarek, do promise," I pleaded, as soon as we were out in the fresh air again.

"You're like this, you are," he said, giving an angry kick to a rotten peach that was lying on the pavement. "How can I tell on you, now that you've pulled me into your rotten mess, too?" He went off without saying good-bye.

I rescued Adler from the saloon, picked up the suitcase, and began to hunt for some quiet corner where there were no people. There I counted the bills into his hand. But he was no longer alive. He was a sort of reeling shadow.

As though he were a deaf-mute, I shouted into his ear: "Eight hundred, Adler. That's an immense sum of money. You can live a year on that."

He simply held the money in his numbed hand. I myself took the wallet out of his coat-pocket and folded the eight bills into it.

Then began the most terrible of all our nights of wandering. What a picture we made! I, with the hand-bag, and the reeling shadow. We went from saloon to saloon. I refrained from drinking much; but, wherever possible, I ordered Swedish punch for Adler. It was a drink of which he had come to be extremely fond.

I was consumed by the idea that I must keep talking incessantly, or I would lose my influence over him and everything might fall through at the last moment. Now, it is hard enough to spend even one short hour with anyone and do all the talking. But at least a living man answers, denies, affirms, assists. But a corpse! And Adler was a corpse now. I had awakened him from death just one brief moment too soon. While I was winning him back to life, his gaze was already directed toward the world of shades. Perhaps he had already pressed too far across the threshold—across the bounds that death has fixed for the soul.

I talked on like one possessed, without so much as a pause. And a terrible desire did possess me to have done with this corpse, with whom I was walled up in one narrow grave.

This weird grave, imprisoning us both, receded on all sides into the smoke and foul air of the café we were sitting in. Our grave was like a hermetically sealed glass bell, smothering us. I would be glad to get rid of this corpse. We must bury our dead. There was nothing wrong about that, it was a universal law, though, of course we must rid ourselves of them in a temporal and not in an eternal sense. But it was only by incessantly talking that I could control this corpse; so that I must not even so much as dream of sleeping. For, after one has slept, everything changes, everything begins anew.

About three o'clock the waiters put us out of the last café.

It was not yet light. I wanted to give God one last chance to save this human soul from me. I remembered that Kio had sent us a message. Perhaps he intended to hush up our crime. Perhaps everything was not quite lost yet. Perhaps we would still be saved by some miracle.

Down the same streets where I had so skilfully followed Kio on the night of our disaster, I now wound my way to and fro with my heavy burdens. What would or could still happen, I was no longer certain. What I was doing was not for myself; it was for Adler. Let God take notice, I was giving Him a last chance.

That hollow, resounding hour between night and morning made Kio's little house in the northern suburb look poorer still, more shabby and older. The scarred paint was peeling off in patches. And here, on the verge of earthly things, a miracle did really happen. For there was a light

in the last window of the third storey right, Kio's window.
Adler knew it at once. Kio was still up, correcting papers.
I seemed to see absurdly clear before my eyes a sentence full
of treacherous pitfalls which Kio must be reading in each
of the twenty-seven note-books: "If Vercingetorix had dismissed his ambassadors, the legate would not have been
able to break up winter-quarters as he had planned."

A soft cry burst from Adler's throat. "Kio!" Then again
and again, "Kio! Kio!" It sounded like the distant cooing
of a hoot-owl. With these birdlike calls, as sad as twilight,
both of us kept calling more and more beseechingly to the
man behind the window.

Then, as our calls echoed along the sleeping street like
cries for help, and were answered by a window indignantly
flung up, Kio turned out his light and went to bed. God
had remained indifferent.

Presently, under the paling sky, under the vengeful gray
dawn of another day, a drab column of men drew nearer.
The street-repairers were beginning their day's work. The
steam-roller puffed and roared in front of them.

I gripped Adler's arm tighter and my tongue kept wag-
ging. Presently we sat down in the park. Through all
eternity I shall remember the bench we sat on. The heavens
were already aglow. It grew lighter and lighter. The light
seemed almost physical, cooling my fever like a chill wind.
In the trees a piercing hubbub of sparrows started suddenly
without warning. The fat ornamental fowls came wad-
dling, like little bourgeois, out of their green coops on the
island in the middle of the pond. Then the swans began
to swim in regal circles before my tired eyes.

Adler's head had dropped on one side. He had fallen

asleep. But it was not heaven's intention that he, any more than I, should sleep. For even those brief minutes during which I had nodded had made him feel stronger. Talk to him, talk to him, I thought. I shook him.

"Your sudden disappearance will cause a sensation in the city," I said. "Marianne will be immensely impressed. She'll fall in love with you immediately. You'll supplant all the others. I'll give you her picture."

How right my instinct had been! After only five minutes' sleep, a changed Adler was sitting beside me. He crumpled up the photograph of Marianne in costume, and threw it angrily on the grass.

"Sensation!" he said. "Only you, only you, would always be seeking sensations!" His resistance was increasing. And there was still a whole hour to wait.

"Of course, we're overexcited, Adler, but you'll soon be sleeping comfortably on the train, while I'm at the faculty-meeting."

"Sleeping?" he said. "Who spoiled our sleeping before, you coward?"

"Why do you scold me? How am I a coward?"

He was triumphant. "Do you think I didn't notice that you got up and ran away, you renegade?"

"How could I have saved you without saving myself?"

"Who gave you any right to save me? Who do you think you are?"

Adler was no longer merely a shadow. This was the same voice that had said to me once long ago, "You ought to be satisfied that you're in the club at all, and wait until a part is given you."

"You're too much of a coward to kill yourself, or anybody else," he said. "Too much of a coward! Too much of a coward!"

I felt weaker and weaker.

"I wasn't too much of a coward to commit a crime for you yesterday, Adler."

He rose and stood tense, towering over me. From his forehead a year-old torpidity seemed to be vanishing. I had never seen him like that before. But I no longer had the strength to rise. His voice became clearer and clearer. "I can't go home now, that's true. I'll have to burn my bridges. I've nothing against that, either; but you had no right to save me, no right. It makes me furious when I think that it was *your* will that I go away. But I'll burn my bridges when *I* want to, and not when *you* do. I'll never give in to you. . . ." He gave a sudden start and ran away.

Everything was lost, if I did not recover my old strength at once. I forced my body to rise as though it were some strange burden that did not belong to me. During the pursuit I had to carry not only the heavy load of my body, but also the weight of the travelling-bag.

Panting, we raced over the gravel-walks, the lawns, down slopes, through the birch-thicket, around the pond and back again. The first sounds of the awakening city, birds twittering, clocks striking the hour, bells ringing, the whistle of locomotives, broke in on us, distorted and exaggerated in the fading darkness.

Above the pond, on a little artificial rock-platform, stood a high, padlocked cage, in which an eagle was imprisoned. There I thought I might catch the fugitive. We raced around the cage. The bird grew excited and began to nip the bars with its beak. It filled the air with a shower of gray feathers and with that bloody, pestilential odor common to all birds of prey.

"Stop, Adler," I cried, as we raced round and round the cage. "I won't hurt you. . . ."

"I'm going home now . . ." he panted out while running. "I'd like to see anyone stop me. . . ."

"Nobody will stop you," I shouted. "Go home. Go to your uncle. Let him get hold of you. . . ."

Then the eagle began to mingle his cries with ours. Finally I succeeded in cutting off Adler's escape, as he tried to dodge to one side. I caught him by the arm. But he seized hold of me and began to press my chest tighter and tighter. God help us! The same struggle we had fought to a finish before was beginning all over again. Suddenly we heard footsteps approaching. "Look out, a policeman!" I whispered hoarsely.

A police-officer really was walking towards us. The sudden thought occurred to me that the police were already in charge of our case. The officer was coming to arrest me. He stopped a little way from where we were standing. He had a good-natured voice and features.

"What's going on here?" he asked. "You two had better move along."

Suddenly Adler burst out into one of his hysterical laughs. The officer frowned. Was it his duty to proceed against such scornful laughter? But, after all, we were only boys, and boys often laughed at him. Besides, it saved him from appearing in court. He turned a deaf ear to us, and his broad shoulders disappeared.

But Adler was still laughing as he let me guide him

again. Presently he grew silent and followed of his own accord.

"After all, what can you do to me, you?" he kept repeating—and there was a new joyous ring in his voice.

I bought his ticket to Hamburg. We entered the waiting-room of the station. Adler sat, hunched over, on my suitcase, like a well-behaved child. When, as a four-year-old, he had been lost in the grain-field, he must have gazed up at the clouds with the same distracted look with which he now stared at the iron ceiling-girders.

Fifteen more minutes and I would be free of Adler for all time. What was there that could still happen in that short interval? My marks in the class-register were not tampered with; and Adler's flight would speak for itself. Hamburg was far away. But suppose he were to come back? No, Adler was a man who would never come back. He would simply disappear forever. And I would be absolved of the guilt caused by my torment and my crime. I would simply have a fainting-fit in school today, and get sick. That would be a splendid turn to give things. A fainting-fit always makes a strong impression; and sickness frightens everybody. My illness would help me over a number of difficult weeks.

Only ten minutes more! My God, my God, if only there were no more accidents, no late train, and no acquaintances to run into!

But God did send one more trial. Komarek suddenly appeared on the platform. He greeted me hostilely. "I've been thinking about it all night," he said, "and I've come to the conclusion that it would be better for you to go and let Adler stay here."

I pulled him to one side, where Adler could not hear us. "For God's sake, Komarek," I said, "you don't know what you're meddling with. You don't know what's happened. Do you want Adler to be put in jail?"

"No, I'd much rather you were."

I answered him proudly. "Well, you'll wait a long time for that. Nothing will be done to me, absolutely nothing. My father is the most powerful judge in Austria."

"That's true," he said, "nothing will be done to you . . . but a good deal will be done to the others. . . ."

I looked at Adler. He was sitting contentedly. My reasoning grew more cogent. "You can see for yourself, Komarek, that if I carry the affair off alone, there's some hope for us. But if Adler stays here, it means the end of everything, and even you'll be glad to come off clean."

"Me? What has your dirty mess got to do with me?"

"I'll tell you in a second, my dear Komarek. Suppose I give back the railroad-ticket. We'll take Adler home, and we'll go to the faculty-meeting at eight o'clock tomorrow morning. By half-past eight a bomb will go off that will be heard from here to Vienna. The net result will be that every undesirable element will be cleaned out of St. Nikolaus with a fine comb. And you can hardly doubt but that you'll be included among the undesirable elements."

Komarek averted his eyes. My reasoning was flawless. "But if they see that conditions in the school are so terrible that one of the students has had to run away, they won't hold us responsible. They'll hold the faculty."

He bared his teeth as he said, "Do you really think so?"

"I know it," I answered. "It's my own scheme. The old teachers will be forced to resign on pension. The younger ones will be punished in one way or another, and Stowasser will be discharged."

"For once the faculty will see how they like it," he said. "It will be fine." A tremendous joy flashed from his eyes. "The dogs!" He could no longer control himself.

Then he walked over to Adler and quickly picked up the suitcase. The train was already whistling into the station. I don't know how he got him into the car. But suddenly they had both disappeared. The train seemed to suck up the throng. Was Adler among those people? I had another anxious moment until I saw Komarek lugging the travelling-bag into a compartment. A minute later he came back and said: "He's already asleep. He's so tired, poor fellow." Then I caught a glimpse, through the dirty train-window, of Adler's slumbering face. Indistinctly I saw that colossal boyish forehead, looking ghastly-yellow under his reddish hair.

"I left him some fruit and sandwiches," Komarek confessed. And then, radiant and proud at the same time, as though to show that what a Komarek had to give was by no means contemptible, he added, "I bought him raspberries."

With my last ounce of strength I stared at the starter, who was giving the signal for departure. As the train-whistle blew, I said: "I can't stand any more, Komarek. . . . I don't think I could stand any more."

Dr. Ernst Sebastian, the examining magistrate, did not know how long he had been asleep in that position, with one arm laid on his desk and his head buried in it. Nor was he quite sure of the time. "Midday sun," he said reflectively, "summer sun, Sunday sun."

How disagreeable to think that the examination would be tomorrow, was his next thought.

Then his eye fell on the sheets of paper lying before him. How could this be? There must be more of them, many more. He had been under the impression that his flying hand had reported his adolescent life from many angles while he was in his trance. Could these few papers be all there was of it? The first few sheets were thickly covered with a shorthand that grew more and more disjointed and confused as it proceeded. Often it seemed to consist of single words, phrases, and short sentences. There seemed to be no regular sequence. Later all kinds of symbols were mingled in the indecipherable text, all sorts of signs, bearded heads, animals' faces, a tree with a garden-bench beneath it, an odd-looking bat. On the white paper, the astonished magistrate read Latin sentences, and chemical formulæ, the word "passed," and other reminiscences of St. Nikolaus Academy.

Then, staring at the sheets before him, he seemed to remember that once, long ago, he used to scribble meaningless words and nonsense. Oh, that perverse habit of his! Even at school he was forever inking up blotters.

He tried to study out the first few lines. They danced before his eyes. These dots, curves, and abbreviations of his own original shorthand rose up and seemed to separate one from another—seemed to become the ancient, mysterious writing of some forgotten people. His own hieroglyphics mocked him. He shut his eyes in an effort to collect his wits. When he opened them again, he saw only birds, noses, utensils, waves, and breasts. He could not understand them now. He pushed the writing to one side.

Then, like a vignette at the end of the last page, he saw a mathematical formula, written large:

$$\sqrt[2]{\left(\frac{\text{Life force} - \text{Perversion}}{\text{Hardening of the Arteries}}\right)}\ x = \text{Death}$$

Sebastian suddenly felt for his pulse. His heart was throbbing wildly and irregularly.

CHAPTER VII

THE examining magistrate, Dr. Ernst Sebastian, arrived at his office a half-hour late on Monday—something that had never occurred before. His clerk, the young lawyer, Doctor Elsner, attributed his lateness to the vile weather they were having that day.

Sebastian belonged to that peculiar type of person that is affected by every change in the weather. He kept a barometer on his desk, by which to gauge the state of his health from hour to hour. His nerves were exquisitely attuned—in the profoundest sense of the word—to the bearableness or unbearableness of life. In this respect, his sufferings had increased with the years. Ah, how rare those moments now were, when life was anything more than just bearable—a soft east wind under a sunny sky, a moderate northwest wind blowing on a fair June day, a few minutes of exhilaration after a thunder-shower, the sea of ozone that lapped the peaks of mountains.

But the weather of late had been really hateful. It required the greatest self-control merely to take a step, or utter a word, or complete work of any kind. It was better to stretch one's self full-length and simply submit to bear in hopeless silence the drab dream that our life may be eternal. The air was like solidifying fat. The city seemed to have been dipped into a cauldron of fat and the lid put on. But some power or other had moved the whole pot too near the fire, so that all the fumes, all the odors, the stenches, the bad breath of the chimneys, the houses, the streets, the depots, and the hundreds of thousands of human lives in them were sucked back down as in a stove whose flues are out of order. "The chill simoon," was Sebastian's rather morbid way of referring to the desperate plight of the world.

As soon as his chief came in, Elsner suggested that he open the window. He had anticipated his chief's feelings.

"Wretch," Sebastian exclaimed, "let it alone!" He shuddered at the thought that the chill simoon might blow into this very office, where, perhaps, there might still be left a little of the atmosphere of better days. It was a long while, a very long while that day, before the examining magistrate gave the usual order: "Tell them to bring in the prisoner, Elsner."

Elsner had risen to obey, when Sebastian called him back from the door.

"What do you think of this case?"

The young man was flattered by so much confidence, and began to speak affectedly. "Well, your Excellency," he said, "what is there to think about it? Adler was the last to leave her room. But, supposing the police have not succeeded in capturing the Feichtinger girl's last client, . . . in that case, I really can't say."

"Do you really believe that this man Adler is capable of committing murder?"

"I know what your Excellency means," said Elsner. "Of course, Adler *is* an educated man, a journalist and an intellectual. But when you study his face more closely, you see that there's a deadly silent look in it that might hide a lot of things. Oh, these intellectuals! In the last few years

we've been through some wonderful experiences with intellectuals."

Sebastian was not satisfied.

"What could be the motive for such a crime? Robbery?
No!—Desire? No!—A passional murder—jealousy, scorned
love, revenge? I think all such motives are out of the question in this case. Besides, Adler had met the Feichtinger
woman only once or twice before in his life. I ask you
again, what could the motives be for such a murder?"

Elsner grew cautious. Did his chief mean to test him
with this question? Had some account of his abilities been
asked for from higher officials? He began discreetly: "If
your Excellency will permit, I would refer you to the
modern methods of analyzing the mind in search of motives
that are not apparent on the surface. . . ."

Elsner was immediately terrified at what he had said. He
had overstepped his mark, for Sebastian declined his suggestion in a very disagreeable way. "For God's sake, let me
alone with your psycho-analysis. I've formed my own opinion already."

The clerk thought that the conversation was ended; but
Sebastian suddenly asked, with a peculiar vehemence,
"Frankly speaking, do you believe he murdered her?"

Elsner tacked about. "I'm inclined," he said, "I'm inclined to think—not."

"Well, I think it's quite possible that he *did*," said Sebastian abruptly.

It's the weather, the young man thought—the weather
and his wretched dogmatism. He heard Sebastian saying,
"Let's begin, please."

Elsner wondered a little that Sebastian did not look at

the prisoner as he sat in the examination-chair, but turned
his glance away from Adler's face in the direction of the
dark little nook between the wall and the bookcases. He
wondered still more that his chief kept using that affected
tone of voice which he ordinarily repressed and used only
in moments of excitement or anger. It was a nasal intonation common to Viennese officials that played nervously, but
exquisitely and insidiously, over his words.

Sebastian had inherited this manner of speaking from his
father, and he fell into it whenever he wanted to conceal
embarrassment or sympathy.

"Good day, Herr Adler," he said. "I suppose that both
of us had time enough to think about each other yesterday.
At least I had. I beg you again, with all my heart, not to
look on me as an enemy. Understand me correctly. I'm
not here to worm my way into your confidence by sly de-
vices of any kind. I want to help you. You won't be any
happier than I will be if the charges against you are dismissed, or at least modified in some way. Let us proceed."

That terrible simoon-headache began to tighten its bands
across his temples. He formulated his first question. "So
you depose that you were Klementine Feichtinger's last
visitor on the night of the murder?"

"How can I say so, your Excellency? I don't know it
myself."

"Of course, of course," Sebastian exclaimed. "You're
right, of course. Naturally you can't know that. . . . Elsner,
it won't be necessary to put that question in the record."

I'm completely muddled, Sebastian thought. That was
the question of an idiot or a half-baked police-investigator.
And Adler suspects there's some trap in it. Every word I

say to him alienates him more. My God, how will I ever reach the end of this hour? His voice confuses me. It has grown deeper. Yesterday I had an entirely different voice in mind.

But the prisoner's voice was pleading: "I'm not guilty, your Excellency."

Sebastian came hurriedly to his aid. "I'm sure you're not, my friend," he said. "But we have to try to make your innocence clear to everyone. And then, besides, there's an endless scale of innocence and guilt. Thank God, our criminal laws draw no more than a tumblerful from the sea of human life." What an absurd comparison, he thought. The sea—a tumblerful! The sea is guiltless. (Third-rate; no talent at all.)

"Under another system of criminal laws," he continued, "I might be sitting before you, as you are now sitting before me. But I didn't mean to go into that. What was it I wanted to say? Oh, yes, I wanted to say that it's quite possible to plead guilty to a crime of which, in the course of the trial, one is proved innocent."

Adler did not seem to follow this train of ideas. "But I have nothing to plead guilty to," he said solemnly.

Elsner kept staring at the point of his pencil, bored and cynical. "This isn't an examination, it's a wild goose-chase," he thought, his pride in his craft offended. "The chief usually lends a willing ear to what they say. I never heard him as bad as this before. He runs on like a phonograph-record, and the prisoner can't get a word in edgewise."

Sebastian took a sheet from the docket and began reading. " 'Klementine Feichtinger was killed by a shot from a revolver. We cite herewith the facts established by the coroner and an expert on firearms. The shot was fired from a distance of two or three feet. The bullet is of the calibre of a seven-millimeter Browning. There were no marks of burning about the wound. Traces of powder could not be established. Consequently suicide appears to be excluded as a motive. Furthermore, a seven-millimeter Browning revolver was found in the possession of the prisoner. One barrel was empty. . . .' I did not by any means consider suicide excluded, Adler," Sebastian broke into his reading. "For example, let us assume, that two persons, say a man and a woman, are tired of life. They decide to die together. It has been done by well-known people before. I'm thinking of Kleist. . . . Surely you dabble a little in prose and verse, Adler, don't you?"

"I did when I was younger," he answered.

"Plays about Frederick and the Church, weren't they? But let's not digress. As I said, two people decide to die. First the woman bares her breast. The man shoots her. The unfortunate woman does not die at once, but suffers agonies which terrify him, which perhaps he has to watch for an hour or more without having the heart to shoot her again. Then, when his turn comes, his own courage has completely oozed away. He has looked on death and he can't go through with it."

Adler kept silent during the pause that intervened before Sebastian resumed: "At this point our criminal laws lag far behind human experience, though in practice they try to overcome the discrepancy. If a double suicide of this type is only half-consummated (and think how often this occurs), the law can render no other verdict but murder.

One can state almost positively that even the prisoner's conscience would say 'No' to a milder verdict. Have you anything to say to me now, Adler?"

The prisoner remained obdurate. "No," he said, "no;
though I can't plead guilty to that either."

"Doctor Elsner," said Sebastian suddenly. "Will you be
so kind as to go up to the chief magistrate's office and ask
personally if there is anything ready for me? And then you
might take a walk for an hour or so, if you like."

Elsner went. Sebastian rose immediately and walked
rapidly and with peculiarly soft footsteps around his desk
and up to Adler. As he spoke, with his strong nasal accent,
allowing no pauses between his words, it sounded as if he
were saying something of no importance whatever, something scarcely worth saying at all.

"Adler," he was saying. "Haven't you recognized me,
too, Adler?" With these words he extended a limp arm,
from which his hand dangled uncertainly. The proffered
hand was not accepted.

"I don't know what your Excellency means . . ."

Sebastian began to run the ends of his sentences together.
He laughed in a hollow way.

"It's been a long time since we parted, eh, Adler? But I
knew that it was you—the day before yesterday."

"But, your Excellency . . . !"

"Stop!" Sebastian ordered. "I'm not your Excellency."

The man leaned heavily on the examination-chair. He
looked unkempt, like all men after their first few days of
imprisonment. He seemed to have grown stouter, too, and
his neck looked fat. The room was full of a depressing gray
light. It was the sort of day when people light lamps at

dinner-time and hope that a thunder-storm won't break. There was no sound in the room but Adler's breathing— the labored breathing of a man who is sick at heart, or who has some heavy load on his chest. With four rapid steps Sebastian walked to the corner by the bookcase. He was not looking at the picture, half-hidden in the darkness, which he had hung there as a warning to himself in dispensing justice. It showed the famous prison-yard at Arles, with the condemned men in lock-step.

Then he saw Adler's broad shoulders trembling like a ship's side in a heavy sea, as he labored for breath.

Sebastian did not stir out of his corner. His voice sounded quite thin as he asked, "Have you any reason for not recognizing me?"

Then the voice that belonged to those storm-shaken shoulders said, "God knows, I have no reason."

Sebastian's answer sought to pierce Adler. "God knows, you *have* reason," he said.

Retreating into his corner, though confronted still by those heaving shoulders, that never once turned round in all their struggles for breath, Sebastian piled sentence upon sentence. "Don't say that we were only boys then, Adler. I won't excuse it that way. Even when a child kills something, it doesn't come to life again. Twenty-five years is nothing. Time is nothing! I've suffered horribly from it. No, I'm not lying to you. Of course, I haven't always thought about it. I haven't even thought about it often; but I've always been conscious of it, Adler, always been conscious of it in my inmost soul. And ever since that day, I've always known that you'd come back, too. Oh, how I've feared your coming! Once a letter came from you. I tore it up without reading it. How glad I was when your mother died, for then the last trace of you disappeared from this city. Do you know that I haven't travelled for twenty years, for fear of meeting you somewhere abroad? Oh, please don't speak; don't say anything yet! This is a terrible moment for me, Adler. I don't understand it myself. I can't solve its mystery myself. It's an equation with a hundred unknown quantities! I'm only talking because I'm too weak to speak the truth. Help me! I beg you, don't listen to my falsehoods, don't listen to the words I'm saying, listen to me, to the real me! And don't say anything; don't say anything yet."

Adler didn't say anything. But his head had dropped forward a little.

"I know what you want to say. I know every objection you'll make. Guilt, you'll say, what is that? We inherit our bodies, our blood, our brains from our forebears. Since we're powerless to shape our destinies, how can we be guilty of shaping the destinies of others? All very well, I know all that. If I hadn't driven you away, sooner or later someone else would, or you'd have done it yourself! Very well, suppose it did come to that! How does that help me, who am guilty of ruining your life? I plead guilty to it. Whatever you may have done, I, and I only, am responsible for it."

Adler pressed his two clenched hands to his head and uttered a dull sound twice. It sounded like "No, no!" Sebastian kept his eyes shut. He was as pale as a drug-addict.

"No. You mustn't say that. Don't say conscience! I haven't got any. I've seen and been through too

much. I'm absolutely conscienceless. Time and again I've
abandoned women, never even troubled myself about the
children I may have had by them. Oh, I've less than no
conscience. I've forgotten them, forgotten their voices, their
hair, their eyes, forgotten them completely, and without a
trace of regret. I would commit murder ten times over
rather than risk a sleepless night. But the fact remains that
you I've never forgotten even for a moment. I plead guilty
to ruining your life. But I charge you, too, with ruining
mine. When we were boys together, your finer nature made
a criminal of me; but when I had driven you away, you
robbed me of my soul for ever. Now, when death seems
ridiculously close to me, I accuse you of ruining my life.
For I was fated to love you!"

Adler's back was humped like that of a buffalo when it
lowers its horns. Sebastian was listening to the sound of
his own words, as though they came from a great distance,
as a dying man listens to the consolations of a priest.

"I know there's such a thing as compensation," he went
on, "but no forgiveness. For compensation is a law. Forgiveness is not. It may be foolish, but I'm going to ask you
for what doesn't exist."

Suddenly Adler leaped to his feet, with a moan that was
also a sob. The examination-chair clattered to the floor.
"For God's sake, I didn't do it!" he shouted.

Then Sebastian shrieked (or was he really singing?), "No,
not you, no, not you. . . ."

The scene that followed was such as this room—with its
ponderous official table, its cases full of law-books, the
examination-chair and all the rest of the pitiless furniture
of justice—was to witness for the first and last time. With

his face distorted, as though in death, the examining magistrate sprang at the prisoner and seized him in his arms. It looked as if a life-and-death struggle were about to begin. But Sebastian's arms slid down from Adler's body. Adler caught him as he was falling, and supported him by the shoulders like a wounded man. In this rigid pose they stood, for a minute or two, like statues. Then the words of an exclamation came rattling from Adler's throat. "But, your Excellency," he said.

Sebastian lifted his head slowly. Who was this man beside him? He was standing still. A frightened face was staring at him in amazement, striving to detect madness or some murderous judicial trick in his features. No, he had never seen that face anywhere before. Had Adler fled suddenly and left this stranger in his stead? His skull was huge and dented. That much was true. He was nearsighted; he wore glasses. That also was true. But the dirty gray hair, which had seemed so red in the sunset on the day of the first examination, now revealed black and white threads.

He had the melancholy and troubled face of a literary man who has succeeded at nothing and has finally stumbled on some severe misfortune.

There was no trace of Adler in that face.

Sebastian turned around and stared out of the window for a little while, in order to recover his breath and compose his mind. He was not entirely successful for some time. He decided to wait another moment or so. Then he tested himself, like an actor before he steps on the stage; he shook himself a little and fled behind his desk with light, almost tripping steps.

"So you don't remember anything about St. Nikolaus Academy?"

"No, your Excellency, on my oath, no."

"But your name is Franz Adler?"

"Franz Josef Adler, of Gablonz!"

Sebastian dropped into his chair and did not take his eyes off the opened docket entitled, "Murder of Klementine Feichtinger, Prostitute."

"Yes," he forced himself to say, "it's true. . . . It's absolutely true. Franz Josef, and Gablonz—they're both stated in your record. Your distinguishing characteristics . . . I've overlooked them or forgotten what they are."

He made an irresolute gesture. It was the politely formal gesture with which we invite a guest to be seated, and seemed totally out of place in that office. The prisoner remained standing, while Sebastian continued his attempts to conceal his embarrassment and fatigue.

"I'm very sorry, my dear Sir," he said, "but what happened just now . . . can't be undone, of course. . . . But I'll have to ask you to forgive and forget it. I had confused you with an old schoolmate of mine, whom you do resemble a little. . . ."

"There are many people with my name," the prisoner murmured, engrossed in his own fate.

Sebastian's voice grew softer and softer. "You understand, of course," he said, "that this remarkable resemblance won't do any harm to your case. I give you my word that your case will be handled with exactly the same consideration as if you really were that person. I wish, however, that you'd be good enough to forget what I said to you about the double suicide. But if you really are innocent, we'll use every means to ... Now, good-bye, and, as I said, forget everything as soon as you can."

Walking backwards, the prisoner retreated from the room. He was overjoyed to get away, although he had resigned himself to undergo the regular examination, which he knew was given to all prisoners. But his manner still betrayed traces of relief and astonishment.

Then Sebastian decided to open the window at all costs. Even though the outer air stifled him, at least it came from the open sky. The street dragged out its weary life below. Its cars, wagons, horses, and humans—all pressed forward with jerky little steps. They all seemed possessed by some impulse to get somewhere where things like themselves did not exist. Only the dogs seemed to lead happy lives, as they chased one another round in circles. The little strip of park opposite the examining magistrate's window was wasting away like a human being. The thick foliage of the trees hung withered, limp, and sere. The dead weight of the atmosphere pressed like a gigantic pillow across the tired and torpid face of life. The street-sounds came up to Sebastian like suppressed chuckles. The atmosphere seemed to be filled with something clotted and curdled. It reminded Sebastian of the banal remarks that clutter some horribly dull conversation. And there was no sign of any betterment on earth, only a universal decay.

When Doctor Elsner next saw his chief, he was hanging with his body half-way out of the window. "It's getting a little better," he ventured to remark.

"I don't notice it," said Sebastian, disdaining the consoling lie.

The young lawyer arranged the pages of the Feichtinger docket. "I heard something in the chief's office that will interest your Excellency a great deal," he said. "The police are on the trail of a later visitor of the murdered woman. . . . There are some new clues. . . . They'll let us know as soon as anything turns up."

Sebastian wheeled around quickly. His mouth hung open for some time before he could utter a word. "So he really was sent in justice as a substitute for . . ." he began.

Before Elsner had had time to reflect on the mysterious meaning of these words, he saw the highly-cultured and reserved magistrate making such motions with his arms as he had never beheld before. Sebastian had raised his arms, and, with his head thrown back, was stretching his hands heavenward. It was the gesture of those Biblical figures we see in old pictures, striving to snatch at the floating robes of the ascending angels. The terror of prophecy glowed like a burning point in space.

For, truly, Sebastian had just experienced one of those moments in our lives that can neither be repeated nor described, when a spark is transmitted from God to man.

But he instantly drew back, ashamed of his ecstasy, ashamed of God, as of a Being in whose company one does not like to be caught in public.

"It's a very remarkable business," he said. "I mistook this Franz Adler for a former schoolmate of mine."

Elsner was surprised. "Why, I could have explained that to your Excellency two days ago," he said. "This man's name is not Franz. They call him 'Cross-Word Josef.' He's a well-known figure in Bohemian cafés and at the Chess Club. I've often seen him there myself."

Sebastian disliked to discuss the matter any further with a subordinate; but, since he had revealed so much already, he might just as well go on.

"We—that is to say, my graduating-class at the Academy —celebrated its anniversary the day before yesterday. Under the spell of that celebration, I must have confused one face with the other . . . which is not so strange after the lapse of a quarter of a century."

"Oh, such things happen sometimes," the clerk agreed.

Sebastian walked up and down the room a few times. He cast a glance at the prison-yard at Arles.

"We must take every care that this man is set free just as soon as anything new turns up. I wish you would telephone for further information today."

"Without fail, your Excellency."

Sebastian's lips repressed a smile that was fast becoming a sneer. He had cleverly succeeded in hiding God's proximity. He would continue to keep it to himself.

"You're an expert stenographer, aren't you, Elsner?" he asked.

"Yes," he said, "I teach it."

"Then it would interest me a good deal to see if you can read even a line of this manuscript."

His hand trembled as he passed Elsner the pages on which he had yesterday scrawled a portion of his life. Or so he thought.

Elsner studied the writing for some time. He held it at arms' length, he took it to the window. Then he brought it back and at last declared that he couldn't make out a single word.

"It's a system I never saw before in my life," he said.

"But, if your Excellency wishes, I'll give it to an expert to transcribe."

Sebastian reached hurriedly for the pages. "That won't be necessary, Elsner. Thank you all the same. I'm quite content if these pages are not too easy to read; for, who knows—after all, it may all be different from. . . ."

He stopped abruptly, and, brushing the sheets together, swept the story of his boyhood crime into one of the side-drawers of his large official desk.

Redwood Library

1. Three volumes may be taken at a time and only three on one share. Two unbound numbers of a monthly and three numbers of a weekly publication are counted as a volume.

2. Books other than 7-day and 14-day ones may be kept out 28 days. **Books cannot be renewed or transferred.**

3. Books overdue are subject to a fine of one cent a day for fourteen days, **and five cents a day for each day thereafter.**

4. Neglect to pay the fine will debar from the use of the Library.

5. No book is to be lent out of the house of the person to whom it is charged.

6. Any person who shall soil (deface) or damage or lose a book belonging to the Library shall be liable to such fine as the Directors may impose; or shall pay the value of the book or of the set, if it be a part of a set, as the Directors may elect. All scribbling or any marking or writing whatever, folding or turning down the leaves as well as cutting or tearing any matter from a book belonging to the Library, will be considered defacement and damage.